HER VOICE, HER STYLE, HER WAY

PRESENTS:

She Got Love For A Bean Town Thug!

BY:

LASHONDA DEVAUGHN

An LSDV Production...

1

D1114235

In Loving Memory of Andre Stone

We did it again baby bro!

Acknowledgements

First and foremost, I'd like to thank GOD for Blessing me with another opportunity to use my craft. I'd also like to thank my family and friends for always being patient with me when I need to isolate myself and get into my writing zone. Your patience is appreciated! To all of my readers new and old, and those of you who have been holding me down since day ONE, all I can say is THANK YOU and I appreciate you all more than you would ever know! Thanks for rocking with your girl!

A major shot out to the ladies of the Queen Pens; Shan, Tamika and Jessica! This group of women couldn't have been any doper and I'm looking forward to touring the world together and inspiring more female bosses!

To all the women out there who have been working on a craft, passion or business and have felt like giving up, hang in there Queen! Use each day to go harder, step outside of your comfort zone, challenge yourself and stay consistent. You may not always win every time, but even the losses are a part of your journey. Use every single part of your experience as a lesson and as fuel to keep going. Push through and continue to believe in your talent even if no one else does. Keep GOD first and remember consistency is key. You are almost there, don't ever give up on your dreams!

Your girl,
LaShonda DeVaughn

Synopsis:

Everybody wants to find true love, right? But what if you've never experienced being loved by ANYONE, how would you ever know if it's real?

Anthony and Lea are brother and sister who were dealt the worst hand when it came to their home life. Being abandoned by their mom as children and raised by their alcoholic father, forced them to seek love from the streets. Lea sought love from the worst type of men around the way and love found Anthony when he met Nicky. Never feeling loved by his mom, Anthony embraced loyalty over all else, especially when he had to fulfill a family member's dying wish. Love was exempt from his plans.

His crew started from the bottom of the barrel in the Boston streets and when he came up with a plan for them to reach the top, everyone's loyalty was tested, even Nicky's. Will Anthony make it out of Boston with Nicky by his side or will he reject her love and choose his loyalty to his sister and the empire he created? Brace yourself, this isn't your typical love story, see love through the eyes of someone who has never felt the beautiful emotion of love before. Your heart will melt as you feel compassion and relate to everyone's backstory. Anthony will quickly become your favorite thug, but some of these characters in question, will soon find out, that the thug life AIN'T for everybody!

She Got Love For a Bean Town Thug!

Anthony

As the officer snatched my arms behind my back and clasped the handcuffs on my forearms, the clanking of the cuffs tightening seemed to be the only noise that I heard amongst all the other bullshit that was going on. Scores of witnesses were watching the dramatic scene play out. Some were being questioned by the local news; who of course brung their cameras to witness my downfall, but most witnesses were outright too scared to give their statements and shied away from the cameras.

My little sister was crying her heart out begging the dominating officers to let me go. "Let him go!! Let my brother go!! Pleaaase!!" She cried. I could hear her yelling, but her words were faint because everything I was hearing was fading out. Two white cops were holding her back by her arms to retain her, but she put up a fight. My little sister was petite but tough as nails; you could tell by her tears that it was hard for her to see her brother being whisked away by the jakes.

I managed to locate my right hand man in the crowd. He seemed to be hoping not to be scoped by the detectives. I saw him tighten the strings on his black Adidas hoodie as he watched from the sideline. Then I spotted my cousin J-Boy slowly descending from the crowd to defray from being questioned or taken into custody.

I couldn't believe everything was coming to an end. Part of me wished that my team was able to save me. I felt like they were turning their backs on me but what was I expecting them to do? They couldn't rescue me from the surrounding ten to fifteen police cars that had my Beamer squared in. This wasn't a fuckin' movie and them niggas wasn't Ranbow. Yet I still couldn't grasp how I got caught, my game was virgin pussy tight, there was no way for the jakes to be on to me.

The officer placed his hand on the back of my waves and before he pushed my head down to place me in the back of the police car, I took one last look at my team; my sister, my right hand man and my cousin who I could still see walking off. My operation was fool proof, I may have been the ring leader but why was I the only one being arrested? There was no other way to answer it; one of them, was a **SNITCH!**

Chapter 1

One Year earlier

"DADDY, get the phone!" My sister yelled out in her annoying high pitched voice. She reminded me of that chick from the movie *Baby Boy*, Taraji; loud and ghetto for no reason.

"Who is it?" Pops pitched from his bedroom where he was laid up with our promiscuous neighbor Trisha.

My sister placed the phone in her petite lap and gave me a daunting attitude face; I knew what all her eye rolling was for. It usually meant that there was another woman on the phone and she didn't want to yell out her name to pops in fear of sloppy ass Trisha causing another scene in our crib.

That bitch Trisha fucked most of the men in our neighborhood but swore that my father was *her* man. Truth be told, that hoe was far from my father's bitch. Pops stayed smashing any woman that gave him the pussy. After my mom abandoned us to marry a rich white man when I was about six and my sister four, my father took the pain out on alcohol and pussy.

In all honesty, I didn't miss much growing up without our mom; my pops did what he had to do to keep us afloat. However, I felt that my sister Lea might've been more affected emotionally without our mom since she was a female, but of course she was too tough to admit it.

"Who is it?" My father yelled out again. Lea palmed her hand over the phone to whisper to me. "I'm just gonna' tell this chick on the phone that he's busy because I swear if Trisha makes a scene in here today, I ain't gonna' be nice this time, I'm gonna' bust her ugly ass." She rolled her neck dramatically.

I chuckled; my sister was always trying to fight somebody. Growing up in a house with just me and pops; all we did was play fight with her so naturally she became a no-nonsense type of chick.

Lea pressed the phone back to her ear, "he's busy right now; he'll give you a call later, okay? Bye!"

She slammed the phone down on the receiver and yelled out, "pops, they said they'll call you back!"

Lea dramatically forced her eyes toward the ceiling and took a seat next to me on our beat up brown pleather sofa that we had ever since we were kids and we watched T.V. She popped the remote control out of my lap and turned to some ratchet reality show and I let my little sister have her way.

Suddenly we heard a loud SMACK coming from pop's bedroom and Lea leaped off the couch like a ninja.

"Yo' Anthony, I swear if this bitch just put her hands on daddy, it's going down!" She said, pounding her fist in her hand.

"Man sit ya' ass down, she didn't touch him." I wearily tossed a pillow at her.

Commotion continued to commence from pop's room. All that was heard was loud hollering and bickering.

"You just put your hands on me Bitch? Put your clothes on and get the fuck out!" Then we heard Trisha screaming, "I know that was another woman on the phone! Who you got calling here for you

12

Thomas, you still seeing other women? Why didn't you get up to go get the phone?"

Lea and I exchanged glances and then she lost it. "Nah' Ant, fuck that!" She automatically snatched out her tarnished golden bamboo earrings and slammed them on top of our old TV. We still had the old fashioned big body TV because we couldn't afford a flat screen. She grabbed her blue head scarf off of the chipped wooden coffee table and wrapped her shoulder length hair with her fingers.

"Lea, stay out of that shit man, he's a grown ass man." I picked up the remote and stretched out on the couch. I was a laid back chill type nigga. My family was my top priority, but shit like this happening in the crib was minor shit. My pops was a grown man; I didn't get in his business when it came to his hoes. As for Lea, she was territorial over pops since he was our only parent and she was not about to let any woman put her hands on him.

Lea rushed on her sneakers and advanced toward my father's room, I knew it was about to jump off. Any time Lea transformed from being loud and obnoxious to not talking at all, that's when you needed to pay attention because there was no stopping her.

"Aw shit man... damn!" I hopped up and rushed behind her but she had already reached my pop's room.

BOOM!

She burst the shallow door wide open.

"You put your hands on my father bitch?!?" Lea scraped a handful of Trisha's hair and forced her head against the wall. Her right cheek melted into the wall and she could hardly scream.

"Aghhhhhhh!" She squealed. Lea squeezed her hair so tight, you could hear it tearing out of her scalp. Trisha had no shirt on and her

13

saggy pancake titties hung to her belly button. She didn't even try to cover them up.

"Get your daughter off me Thomas!" She hollared with her eyes squeezed shut holding on to Lea's hands trying to release them from her hair.

My father slid his shorts on under the sheets. "That's enough Lea!" The bass in his voice echoed the room. "Let her go!" He demanded.

With her face tensed tight, Lea yelled all types of shit in Trisha's ear. Of course Trisha didn't try to fight back, she allowed my sister to dominate her. If she would have started swinging, Lea's little ass would have molly-wopped that hoe.

Lea positioned Trisha's head toward hers and locked eyes with her. Trisha was shaking and scared.

"Listen to me real good Trisha because this is your final warning. You come back over here putting your hands on my father or questioning him like you are his fucking wife again, I'm gonna' do more than pull your hair out, I'm gonna' rip out your fuckin' eyeballs bitch."

I laughed because the shit was funny to me but Lea was dead serious. I walked over and pulled my sister off of her. "Come on Lea that's enough man, she's leaving."

I looked Trisha square in the eyes, "right?" I asked her sternly.

With fear in her moist eyes, she answered, "yeah. Yeah, I'm leaving Ant." Lea released her and Trisha swiftly tiptoed around us to find her clothes. Finally she covered her nasty titties with her blue, holey wife beater.

14

"Both of y'all get out of here, this is my business!" My father barked trying to find a clean shirt amongst the pile of musty clothes on his bedroom floor. The room smelled like old people's ass and I could tell by pop's demeanor that he was still drunk because all of his words were slurred. His afro was smooshed on one side and his beard was beaded and un-groomed. If he wasn't my pops I would have easily confused him for a crack-head. But that was my nigga.

"Pops keep your hoes in check, I'm sick of this shit." I preached as I yanked Lea's wild ass out the room with me.

There was always some drama going down at the crib. Whether it was my pops and his many women or my sister who had so much mouth that girls would follow her home to try to jump her. But me? I just maintained. I never brought any of my drama to the crib. I got into little dumb shit on the streets but I was blessed never to get caught doing any of the dirt I had done. In my younger days, I did dumb shit just because I was bored. Shit like stealing cars, shoplifting in corner stores around the way, nickel and diming trees and the occasional fights and shit with the local tough guys. Other than that, I was good in my hood, all the gangsters respected me and all the hustlers did too.

Everyone knew my pops. He was a hot head back in the day. Rumor had it, he caught a bunch of bodies out in Brockton but he was never convicted and till this day he never told me about all the dirt he did. It was the streets that put me on to his past although I could never get the real story out of anyone. Whatever my pops did, I was good everywhere I went.

My right hand man Terror was a different story. Most of the shit that I got into was because of this nigga. He was fascinated with stealing cars and buying guns. He got caught twice for driving stolen vehicles and had to do time in juvey back in the day. Doing time wasn't a threat to him, he was an outlaw, he didn't' give a fuck about anything but fast action. His mother and father was cracked out somewhere in Dorchester so he grew up with his grandmother in Roxbury down the street from where I stay.

Then we had my cousin J-Boy who was the only outside family that I had. Well so I thought. I found out only two years ago that J-boy's mom wasn't really my aunt. She and my mom were best friends back in the day and she felt bad that my mom abandoned me and Lea so she tried her best to be there for us. However, she had her own son to think about so she fell back from us now that we were in our twenties. Me and J-Boy still claimed each other as cousins though. I would die for that nigga.

J-Boy was a so-fresh and so-clean type nigga. The nigga was broke as shit but tried to dress like he was rich. I always clowned him about the tight ass skinny jeans he always rocked with high top bootleg Balenciaga sneakers. This nigga would rock cardigan sweaters over his white tees with fitted hats over his dreads to match his kicks. He was a fake hood-rich type nigga but he was cool to be around to pull shorties because they loved him.

Other than J-Boy and Terror we hung around crazy ass Leon. He was the type of nigga that just lived for the moment. Straight reckless and crazy as fuck! He too came from a broken home. His moms was cracked out and never came around too often so he never claimed her especially since she never did shit for him. And when his mom told him that his pops was gay, he hated him and didn't claim him either. He didn't miss a chance at calling his father a faggot or a fuck-boy. His family situation was all fucked up which is why he always did crazy shit. Whenever some drama popped off in the hood with us, Terror always had a supply of burners but Leon was most likely the one who would use them.

Everyone always compared me to the rapper T.I. I'm not the tallest nigga around but I'm a motherfuckin' boss. I was always the leader, the boss, the nigga who everyone looked up to in my crew. I didn't have to wave guns around and claim a set for niggas to respect me. I had a natural aura of realness that people took to. I was cool with a lot of niggas and I didn't have too many enemies. But growing up in the hood, of course I had a few. No matter how laid back I was, I was fearless and not afraid to put in work if necessary, I mean, I lived in the hood so of course shit happens. So automatically to society, I was labeled as a thug.

I think I got my laid back ways from pops. I was quiet but was quick to pop off when it was necessary. As far as bitches was concerned, I treated them like my pops treated em'. I'd only fuck em' and leave em'. I never had a girlfriend in all of my twenty-three years of living. I didn't trust women. Shit, if my moms could leave her two kids, her own flesh and blood to run away with some dude, then a bitch can do the same to me. So I didn't trust bitches at all. The only female I respected was my little sister Lea.

I held her at a higher standard than any other female. I treated her like she was my daughter although we were only two years apart. I would smack a bitch for my sister and kill a nigga for her. And she would do the same for me. That's why when I peeped her getting out of this nigga who I had beef with for years' whip, I almost lost it on her. I was on my way to meet Leon when I saw my sister with that bitch nigga Donte.

Donte was a local pimp who had been my arch enemy for years. When I ever saw Lea get out of his car, I almost let off on him in broad day because I was wrapped up. Lea was smiling and giggling like they just had a witty conversation. My facial expression was tensed and full of wrath watching them. When she bent to kiss him goodbye, I lost it!

17

I hopped out of my car and sped toward her, going ham with every step I took!

"Lea, get your dumb ass over here! Fuck you doing?" I rashed out!

She shut the door to his Blue Cadillac Deville and spotted me. Her heart was probably beating out of her purple tank top. Donte looked my way with a shady smirk. Nigga was the only clown in the hood that still had braids. And the shits were messy and ungroomed. He turned up his music and then smiled before peeling off.

Lea had her hands up treading toward me. "What? What's wrong with you Ant?" She knew damn well she was out of order.

"What the fuck you doing with that nigga? He pimpin' you too!" I griped.

She rolled her big eyes and I yanked her by the arm when she got closer to me. "Yo', if that nigga is tryna' pimp my little sister, I swear I would murk his whole fam' and I put that on my life!" I let go of her arm and snatched her by her ponytail.

"Let go of me Ant, he ain't pimping me, I ain't stupid! Let go!" She shouted, trying to fight her way out. I hemmed her up to my car and her feisty ass kept trying to fight back like I was a stranger in the street. She was punching and kicking until she lost her energy. With ease I handled her, tossing her against my car without trying to hurt her but enough to contain her. "Ouch Ant! You just broke three of my nails!" She screamed. The acrylic had broken in the middle of her nails and it looked painful. She placed her bent, bleeding, broken fingernails into her mouth. "Fuck ya' nails!" I opened my car door and pushed her into the passenger seat.

I jogged over to the driver's side and got in. "Yo', if I catch that nigga around here again, I'm setting it." I pointed in her face.

"Setting it for what Ant? He was just giving me a ride back from doing my homegirl's hair!" She sassed me.

"So you kiss every nigga that gives you rides?"

She looked down at her lap realizing that I caught her locking lips with that bitch nigga and just thinking about it had me wanting his head.

Our backstory is complicated. Donte and his cousins jumped me in high school and I ended up stabbing him at a house party last year. Every time we saw each other, we were at each other's neck. Lea had never been disloyal EVER, that's why it bothered me to see her around that nigga. She knew how deep our beef ran. Most of Lea's home girls were on Donte's dick because of all that pimp money he made. Truth be told, her girls were just a bunch of hood rats. Don't get me wrong, my sister was hood as shit too but I refused to put her in the hood rat category, she deserved better than a nigga like that.

I gotta' give it Donte though; he was one of the only niggas in the hood really doing it almost better than the drug dealers. But the nigga had the nerve to try to have my little sister in his whip? That shit wasn't riding with me and I blew a fuse!

"Listen to me real clear Lea, the situation you got going on with that nigga better be deaded ASAP or it's gonna' be a problem. You know I got drama with that nigga. It ain't real for you to be out here chilling with the opps!"

She sucked her teeth, folded her arms and chomped down on her gum. Then finally, after all the huffin' and puffin', she popped back at me with the highest attitude in every word. She shifted in the passenger seat to face me. "Yo', y'all had beef in high school, I thought that shit was deaded by now Ant. It ain't that serious, shit!"

"How the fuck is it deaded when you know I stabbed that nigga last year. Shit, Leon was just shooting at one of them niggas the other day. That beef is still on, don't act stupid!"

She rolled her eyes again. "Well no one told Leon's crazy ass to be shooting at nobody. He needs to grow up, y'all had beef in high school, why carry it out? Y'all are adults now, damn!"

"Yo', you heard what I said." I stated firmly. "You hear me?" I confirmed.

"Alright, alright!" She snapped finally caving in. She reached into my dash to pull out some napkins to wrap up her bleeding nails, there was so much blood, you'd think she lost a finger.

Knock! Knock! Knock...

Leon knocked hard on my passenger side window catching both Lea and I both by surprise. Lea manually rolled down the window in my black 1990 Honda Civic because my shit didn't have power locks.

"Nigga don't be popping up out the cut like that, what's good with you?" I asked.

Dressed in the same black Adidas hoodie he wore almost every day because Boston was big on Adidas and Timberlands, and a pair of faded blue Levis, Leon bent his head into the window. "Ain't shit my nigga." He smiled revealing his large yellow teeth. He nodded at Lea, "I just saw you getting out of that nigga Donte's car, what's up with that?"

"None of your business!" Lea snapped rolling her eyes and neck.

"Man fuck that nigga, she know better, I was just in here scolding her about that shit just now." I cut in.

Leon stood tall in his tan Timberland boots and stepped away from the car and lifted up the bottom of his hoodie. "You know I got the hammer on deck for them niggas." He said grinning, revealing his gun tucked in his pants.

"Ohhhh boy." Lea said rolling her eyes hardcore. She placed her broken fingernails back in her mouth. They still hadn't stopped bleeding.

"Yo', as long as he stay away from my little sister and his niggas stay in their lane, it is what it is." I said.

"You already know my nigga." Leon agreed.

I had almost forgot what I was meeting Leon for because I was so pissed off at Lea. "Oh, nigga what you said you wanted again?"

"Give me a twenty bag." He bent his head back into the passenger side window.

I paused. "Nigga you got me out here meeting you for a punk ass twenty bag?"

"Shit, a nigga is down bad right now. I'm thinking about catching me a lick so I can come up dog."

I nodded and reached in my pocket for the weed. "You, J-Boy and Terror need to get y'alls weight up, can't be out here broke man."

"Shit, well find me a job then nigga." He said sarcastically.

"Find yourself a job nigga." I joked back. "Shiiit, I'm on the come up too." I said.

Lea interrupted. "Can we hurry up and go!"

We both looked at her.

"Man be easy, we leaving now with ya' big head ass." I pushed her head into the head rest and leaned over and gave Leon dap exchanging the twenty bag of weed and taking his money.

"A'ight my G, hit me up." I started my car.

"One." He said.

Before he walked away, he looked at Lea. "Bye Mrs. Donte." he joked, always on his slick shit.

"Shut up nigga." Lea swiftly rolled up the window on him. We still heard his raspy laugh when the window was all the way up.

I peeled off and rode up to Joe's sub shop in Dudley to grab me and Lea a steak and cheese sub. I was hungry as shit because pops never kept food at the crib. I grabbed us both a sub, fries and some Arizona iced teas. On the way home, we were joking about the situation that happened at the crib earlier with pops and Trisha. And as usual, we were back to normal as if the whole Donte shit never happened. That's how it was with me and my sis; no one was able to come between us, she was my nigga.

As we walked in the crib, it seemed as if the tension inside was razor sharp. I had never seen tears in my father's eyes before, EVER. He and Trisha were sitting in the kitchen at the small, wooden, square table looking over three sheets of white papers.

"Pops you good?" I asked him placing my sub on the table. The fear that congregated in his eyes when he peered up at me was unforgettable. Never had I seen him look so broken, it appeared as if he was preparing to lose a limb. Trisha's face shared the same mask of worry. Her hands were violently shaking.

Lea and I exchanged glances and we stood confused wondering what the fuck was going on and the suspense was killing us.

"What happened pops, what that hoe do to you now?" Lea pitched. She was staring at Trisha awaiting pops to give her the green light to dig in her ass.

"I'm afraid what she's done this time can't be undone." Pops whispered, sinking his head back down into the papers. He was browsing through the material, sheet after sheet when tears began to pour down his face.

Lea bucked her eyes and we exchanged intense glances again. Pops crying was something that we both had never seen before.

"What are you reading pops? What do you mean what she did can't be undone! Tell me what this bitch did to you?" Lea demanded.

When pops didn't answer, Lea began taking off her earrings and unzipping her jacket. She threw her jacket on one of the empty kitchen chairs and once I didn't hear her say anything else, I knew she was about to go ham.

"Fuck this!" She barked. Lea didn't wait for my pops to answer, she leaped over the table and snatched Trisha by her hair and started pounding her in the face and screaming out loud.

"What the fuck did you do to my pops bitch? How you gonna' have my pops in hear crying, you nasty, fuckin', slut?"

Pops jumped out of his seat to pull Lea off of Trisha. "Stop, don't touch her!" He shouted.

He managed to pull Lea off of Trisha and Trisha remained on the floor crying loudly. Lea had really fucked that lady up, with her broken nails and all. Pops pulled Lea up and rammed her back to the wall. He purposely locked eyes with her for about sixty seconds straight and then started hugging her tightly. His cries were so loud, they echoed the room.

I expelled hard steps towards him. "Pops, what's good? What's wrong with you, why the fuck you crying, what's going on, man?" I begged for answers, I was straight confused. Shit was crazy!

Pops looked at me with an expression that I'd never forget. His eyes were wallowed in tears. "I love both of y'all with every fiber of my being, always remember that. I broke my back to provide for you two and I would do it all over again if I had to. But I will never let anything or anyone have control over my fate except me!" He pat his chest with his fist, hard as fuck.

Lea was breathing heavily from the scuffle and we both stood in the state of massive confusion. That bitch Trisha was still on the floor crying and shaking. She began rocking her body back and forth as her cries grew louder.

"Thomas I'm sorryyyy!" Her cries elevated. Pops turned to look at her with a disheartening look on his face before retreating to his bedroom. Within seconds, he returned to the living room with his chrome 9mm in his hand and he put it at Trisha's temple.

"Pops, what are you doing!" I hollered.

BOOM!!! He let off one shot into Trisha's head and her body fell flat onto the carpet.

Instantly I snatched up Lea and forced her behind me against the wall to protect her because I didn't know what type of shit my pops was on.

He turned toward us with tears pouring out of his eyes like streams. He didn't seem like himself, he seemed to be living outside of his body at the moment. "I love y'all." He said, his voice was cracking and he had the gun at his side. His eyes met mine before he continued. "Anthony, I need you to always protect, love and take care of your sister, always, no matter what." He turned away from us toward the other wall and then without hesitation, BOOOOM!! Pops let off a shot into his own head, execution style. His eyes rolled to the top of his head and then he collapsed to the floor.

"WHAT THE FUCKKKK!!!!!" I shouted. "WHAT THE FUCK!" I repeated, shouting louder. Shit felt like a dream! I couldn't get anything else out of my mouth. My eyes were frozen wide open! I couldn't move, I couldn't believe what the fuck just happened.

"Daddyyyyyyyy!!!" Lea screamed. The sadness in her cries made tears collect at mine. She ran from behind me and knelt down to my father's dead body. She clutched him and soaked his wife beater with her tears and in return, her shirt became drenched in his blood.

She cried hysterically over his body screaming and asking him not to leave us. "Daddy, Daddy, why did you do this Daddy? Please wake uuuuppp! Whyyy did you do this Daddeeeeee whyyy!!! We need youuuuu! What are we going to do without you dadeee? Please wake up, I need my daddyyyy!!" Tears and snot collaborated on her face as she rocked pop's body back and forth.

Frozen in the same spot, I found myself not responding. My heart was racing and my hands were shaking out of control but I couldn't move. I peered over at Trisha on the floor, she was dead but her eyes were still opened. I looked back at my sister and it dawned on me that she was really holding the body of my dead father. Pops was dead and this shit was all real.

Lea raised her head at me with the saddest eyes, "Daddy's gone. He's dead Anthony!!! Why would he do this, why would he leave us like this Anthony, huh? Whyyyyy? He's all we gooottt!!" Her cries were breaking me down. "Not daddy Anthony, I love him soo much! What am I gonna'

25

do without my daddeee?" She sounded just like she did as a little girl. She cried so hard, she lost her breath. Drool was falling out of her mouth onto pop's wife beater and her desperate, grieving cries kept growing louder. The blood from pop's wound was now leaking onto her thighs.

I was still in shock and I couldn't say shit or do shit. My stomach was in knots and I kept wondering when someone was going to wake me up from this nightmare. I smoothed my hands over my face as I looked around. The room was now spinning in both slow and fast motion. Tears were formed at my eyes but I couldn't cry. I couldn't feel anything, all I felt was confused and I didn't know what move to make next. I ran over to the table to grab the papers that pops was reading and what I read made my stomach drop even further to the floor. Swiftly, I slammed the papers back onto the table and shouted toward Lea.

"LEA!! Don't touch him! Don't touch none of the blood. Those papers said that he was HIV positive! Trisha must've infected pops, that's why he killed her first." I finally gained clarity as to why pops just did what he did.

"What?" Lea asked removing pop's bleeding head from her lap. She took off her jeans that were soaked in pop's blood and ran to the bathroom to wash her hands. She threw on some jogging pants and a clean white T-shirt and returned to the living room.

"What the fuck Anthony? This shit is crazy! What are we supposed to do now?" She sadly grabbed her hair with both hands and her baby face wore the saddest face she'd ever shown.

"I don't know sis. I don't know." I nodded as I embraced my baby sister.

It was true, I didn't know what we were going to do or how we were going to live; pops was the one who held us down. I was now forced into a position where I was going to have to do what I had to do, there was no way I would let my pops die in vain, I had to hold my sister down, period. After all, we were truly all that we had now, literally....

Chapter 2

I didn't say much of shit to the police. I hated 5-0! The police brutality in Boston was insane. They used to get away with beating down niggas for no reason. Furthermore, they used to beat my pops up all the time on the streets for being drunk in public. Now that he was dead, I had an even deeper hate for them and anyone else who wronged my pops in the past for that matter.

"Young man, I'm going to need you to answer some more questions."

I glared at the old black cop, I didn't have any more answers to give him; it was what it was; pops shot Trisha and took himself out.

"So your father killed Trisha Waterson and then turned the gun on himself?"

"YES." I answered for what seemed like the fiftieth time.

"Were you or your sister involved in anything pertaining to the crime?" He asked with his pen and pad ready to write some shit down to convict me or Lea.

I took in a deep breath and bit my bottom lip because I wanted to knock this nigga out. "Yo', I just told you everything that happened." I balled my fist and grew extremely frustrated after that. Reality then sank in heavily, pops was gone and I was now the man of the house and the one who had to take order. I demanded that the detectives finish taking pictures and whatever else they had to do on the crime scene and get the fuck out of my house.

After ten minutes, I had to give them niggas another reminder, I was done with this shit.

"A'ight, y'all got what y'all need, like I said, get out! Have some respect; don't ask me or my sister anymore questions, my fuckin' father just died right in front of us and y'all still in this bitch taking your time? Get out!"

The officers and crime scene detectives respected my wishes and shortly after, the house was cleared out.

Lea was planted on the couch crying and I was sitting in the same kitchen chair that my pops was sitting in reading the papers about his death sentence before he killed himself. I had nothing figured out, no plan and no next step. I knew I couldn't pay our rent off of my weed sales. I didn't know what the fuck I was going to do and I couldn't clear the fog out of my mind to come up with something. All I knew was that I had to take care of Lea, by any means necessary.

Knock! Knock! Knock!

I grabbed my gun that I had hidden deep into our dropped ceiling so that the police couldn't find it when they were at my crib and I ran to the door and put one eye to the peep hole. It was Terror, J-Boy and Leon. I had text them and told them what happened with pops. I widened the door and they all walked inside with their heads down.

"Yo', sorry about what happened dog." Leon said dapping me up. Terror and J-Boy also spilled out their condolences. They made their way into the living room and sat down next to Lea on the couch. She immediately shot up and emerged to her room. The way her personality was set up, she hated to show weakness.

The three of them looked over at the blood stains on the carpet and shook their heads. Terror made slow treads over to where the blood was on the carpet and put his hand over his chest.

"Rest in peace pops." And then he raised his hand to his head to salute him.

He took a seat on the couch next to the duo.

"Dog, as soon as I got your text about what happened to your pops, I made the bitch that I was fuckin' put on her clothes and leave my crib." Leon said. We all stared at him in unison; we didn't know what the fuck he was talking about.

"What?" I asked with my brows bent.

"I'm serious, fuck that! I made that bitch bounce! I don't trust no bitch no more. Your pops went out like a G Ant. If a bitch gave me the monster, I would've killed her AND her whole family before I took my life. That shit is disrespectful."

"Man shut up!" J-Boy interrupted. "You're being disrespectful right now nigga," he barked. "He was like my pops too." J-Boy stated in a serious tone.

"Man whatever." Leon said waving him off not realizing his own ignorance. "Shit, he was like my pops too at the end of the day. I never really knew my faggot ass father! I ain't being disrespectful, I'm just saying, I would've killed the bitch too for burning me." Leon defended.

"A'ight nigga, we get it. We don't wanna' hear no more." J-Boy dismissed him.

"Yo, Ant, you straight?" My right hand man Terror asked after seeing me drifting away. I was in a trance, staring off into space. I couldn't even hear what J-Boy and Leon were going at it about anymore, nor did I care. "Yo', yo', Ant, you good?" Terror asked again.

I shook it off and tuned back in. "Nah dog, I ain't good. I'm over here all the way fucked up my dude."

"Well I brought over some smoke and some henny." He pulled out the rollies from his hoody and placed them on the coffee table. As he sparked one up, J-Boy and Leon retreated to the kitchen to get cups for the henny.

"Yo'?" Terror called out to me while he was in between puffs. "It's time for us to make some real money out here dog. This shit ain't a game no more especially now that you have to hold Lea down. I got a connect with these Dominicans for some weight, that weed shit is cool, but you already know there's more bread in white. I can get some doe up so we can go half on a key."

"Man that shit's too risky, if I get locked up, then what Lea gonna' do nigga?" I questioned.

"Yeah, yeah, you right." He agreed. "But just think about it; the connect is on deck, so we good."

"Yeah a'ight." I brushed him off.

J-Boy and Leon re-entered the living room and poured themselves some henny. They filled my cup to the brim because niggas knew I needed it. We smoked and drank till I couldn't feel any more pain. But as soon as my homies left, I locked myself in the bathroom and stared at myself in the mirror. That's when reality hit harder than ever.

I swear it felt like I had the weight of the world on my shoulders. I rubbed my hand over my face and finally started bawling. I can't front, I was crying like a bitch! I forcefully punched the air to let out aggression and I repeatedly paced the small bathroom back and forth talking to myself. I kept seeing visions of pops shooting himself in my head and I kept hearing his voice telling me to take care of Lea.

"Damn, pops. Damn, man!" I cried out trying to gain control of myself. My mind was in total anarchy, I almost punched holes in the bathroom walls but I didn't want to actively show my pain for Lea's sake so I kept throwing blows in mid-air to help release the pain I felt. "Pops, nigga, why did you do this shit to me man, why you leave me out here!" I cried.

Suddenly I stopped pacing the room and I put my fist to my mouth and bit down trying to stop my cries. I looked around the bathroom. Pops dirty wife beaters were all over the floor, his razor was on the sink and his wash rag was still inside the shower. I couldn't believe I wasn't ever going to see him again. I wanted to hurt someone. I wanted to do something severely extreme to take away the pain. It hurt so fuckin' bad, I never felt so defenseless; I was completely torn apart.

Lea knocked on the door, "Ant you okay?" I quickly wiped my tears and cleared my throat. "Yeah I'm good. What's up?"

"Um, when you're done, come into the living room, we got company."

I had no idea who could be visiting us. We didn't have family, pops was our only family and my niggas had just left. From the sound of Lea's tone, whoever it was, she was surprised to see them too.

I maintained my composure, wiped my eyes and entered the living room. Standing before me, dressed in what seemed to be some expensive ass couture shit was none other than my mother. She was beautiful, just as I remembered when I was a shorty. She resembled the singer Aaliyah, light skin complexion, big brown beautiful eyes and long black hair. It was crazy because although I couldn't see any resemblance of myself, she was the splitting image of Lea. I stood against the wall beside Lea and we were both speechless. Our mother was literally a stranger to us. We looked like two homeless kids standing in front of a super star.

She was dressed in an immaculate red cashmere dress suit with black heels with red bottoms and behind her, was her husband looking like a white Rico Suave leaning against the opposite wall with dark black Ray Ban sunglasses on and his hair slicked back. Nigga was suited up looking like he worked for the secret service, standing there straight looking like money.

My mom approached us with sympathy in her eyes.

"I'm so sorry about what happened to your father." Sincerity seemed to linger in her tone; her voice was soft and melodic just as I had remembered it as a kid. She bent to hug Lea first. Lea kept her hands at her sides and didn't hug our mom back. When she hugged me, naturally I did the same thing. I couldn't bring myself to hug her back. Her sympathy to me was fake and unauthentic. Her perfume even smelled expensive and I was fuckin' offended. She looked like she belonged on the cover of a magazine and there we were standing in front of her looking like damn rag dolls compared to her and her husband.

"All these years and you come to visit once pops dies?" Those were the only words that left Lea's mouth. My mom pierced her lips together, rubbing in her red lipstick and then shamefully bent her head down toward our dingy carpet.

"I-I'm sorry, I never meant for it to be like this, I love you both so very much..." She began.

I stopped her. "You love us, huh? That's why you left us, right?" I asked before I nodded. "How did you find out about pops anyway? Why are you here? Who contacted you?" I bombarded her with questions.

"J-Boy's mom called me... But listen babies, I really didn't mean for it to be like this, I swear."

Lea's face was covered with years of built up anger and she took slow steps toward our mom's face. "So what did you mean it to be like then, *mom*? You left us in the hood so you can run off with Hugh Heffner back there and live the good life! Well guess what *mom*? My father had to teach me how to wear a tampon, *he* did my hair when I went to school and *he* had pep talks with me about boys. You ain't my mother. Lady, you're a stranger, we don't know you. Matter fact, get the fuck out of my house!"

My mother lifted her face up to explain herself but Lea smacked the dog shit out of her, forcing her head back.

"Uhhh!" My mother held her cheek and her eyes formed tears. Her slow gaze into Lea's eyes left Lea unmoved. "You have the same fight in you that I have; you're just like me when I was your age."

"I ain't shit like you lady, pops was my mother *and* father. I don't even know you. Take your meal ticket back there and both of y'all get the fuck out!" She demanded.

Mom tucked in both of her lips as tears continued leaving her beautiful brown eyes.

She sniffed. "Larry, give them the envelope, let's go." Still holding her cheek, she turned my way, "I love you Anthony, always will. I'm sorry about your father and I'm sorry for leaving you both and I hope one day you will understand why." I didn't say shit back to her. If I was to speak, my words would've been pure disrespectful. How could someone leave their children and appear well over a decade later after our guardian dies? I had absolutely no words or respect for this woman; she deserved more than a smack from my little sister.

In tears, my mom left the apartment in a hurry. Her husband Larry tried handing me a white envelope but I mean mugged that nigga and didn't take it. He placed it on the kitchen table, fixed his Burberry tie and marched out behind my mom.

Lea stormed off to her room and slammed the door loudly. That was actually the first time that I'd ever heard her express what she was missing out of her life from not having our mom present. Deep down, I always knew it ate at her but she never expressed it. She was always so hardcore and expressed her anger in different ways.

Standing there alone, I took a deep breath and looked around. The apartment now felt so lifeless and cold. The sense of emptiness was especially overwhelming, when I looked over at the blood. It almost felt like I wasn't there. Losing pops, seeing my mom for the first time in years and realizing that I didn't have room in my heart to forgive her, filled my insides with even more grief. Not to mention the heavy burden of having to provide for Lea was over my head. If I had to put my life on the line, I'd do it for my sister. By any means necessary...

I woke up the next day with the same sense of emptiness. I didn't feel like myself at all, all the pain made my body ache. The apartment was mute and it smelled lifeless and eerie. Upon entering the living room that morning, I stared at the couch and shook my head slowly. Usually pops would be up early in the morning laid back on the couch smoking a cigarette and watching TV with a holey T-shirt on wearing the same gray jogging pants that he died in. Some chick would be leaving out of his room with her hair undone from getting her back blown out and I'd always chuckle because the shit was routine for him.

Suddenly I wondered how long my father was HIV positive and how long Trisha kept it from him. I'd hoped he hadn't infected any other women and his situation just made me not trust women even more. I was already scarred from my mother's mistakes, now pops added to my resistance towards trusting bitches even more.

Suddenly I felt Lea walking up behind me. Her brown face was red and puffy and her cheeks were saturated with tears. She stared at the empty couch with me and then held out her arms for me to embrace her. "Ant this is real, daddy's really goneeeee! I will never be able to get through this. Never!" She choked on her cries. I squeezed her tight and calibrated my emotions while her tears of grief soaked my black shirt.

"We gonna' be good Lea. I promise." I assured her.

Slowly, she turned away from the couch to face the blood on the floor and she instantly started gagging. She bolted to the bathroom and I heard her vomiting into the toilet. Sharing her pain, my stomach instantly grew weak when I turned to look at the blood stained carpet again. This wasn't supposed to happen! Pops wasn't supposed to give up like this, knowing that he was all that we had. The blood hadn't even dried, the carpet was still moist and red. It wasn't red like the blood in the movies, it was more like a burgundy color and it felt surreal looking at it because I had never saw a dead person's blood before. It angered me when I thought about my father taking his own life even before the poison that consumed his blood.

Lea returned from the bathroom with two bottles of bleach and we poured it over the blood stains and covered them with sheets. We didn't want to touch the blood nor did we want to be reminded of what happened the night before. Honestly, we didn't know where to begin with picking up the pieces of our lives without pops.

Silently we sat on the couch for like an hour straight. Lea laid her head on my shoulder like she used to when we were kids and I just stared out in the air in deep thought. I tried tirelessly to fight through the grief but it was too hard. I cried silently, while Lea continued to cry out loud. Neither one of us brought up our mom and the fact that she popped up after not seeing her in years. But honestly, it was always a subject that we never really touched. She too, was dead to us.

I literally felt like our situation was out of my control and I had to gain some sort of grasp on it and the time was now. I decided that I couldn't continue to watch us deteriorate, I had to get us out of the house. Staying inside was too painful. I convinced Lea to get dressed so that we could go get something permanent in pop's memory; some tattoos. She re-wrapped her broken nails with gauze and medical tape and got dressed.

I went outside to start the car and she met me there, painfully taking steps to the passenger side of the car. My baby sister looked like a zombie sitting next to me. She was staring out onto the road blankly and it was killing me to watch her in so much pain.

I drove us straight to the tattoo shop and parked on the side of the building. I planned to get my pop's face tatted on my chest and Lea said she wanted to get a red rose with a band showcasing his name on her arm. I stared at my sister and grabbed her hand before we got out of the car. Our eyes were puffy and we looked like dog shit, but we were gonna' get through this together.

"What pops used to say to us? Y'all are a team, 'Ant and Lea'." I kissed her hand.

"Ant and Lea." She repeated, squeezing my hand tighter before we exited the car.

Thankfully we were the first customers in the shop so we were able to be seen right away. A familiar looking Puerto Rican dude slipped on his latex gloves after sketching out my father's face on the cray paper from the photo that I had given him. He motioned for me to lay back on the long, black leather recliner. I laid flat on my back and got ready to get inked up.

"You live over there in them apartment complexes in Warren Gardens, right?" He spoke to me as he prepped me for my tattoo.

"Yeah why, where do I know you from?" I asked wondering how the fuck the nigga knew where I lived.

"Oh nah, we don't know each other, but I seen you around before. I used to live in Warren Gardens for about two months but the crime was too crazy so I moved to the South End." He shook his head. "Matter fact, I just heard about some crazy shit that happened up there just yesterday, some nigga killed some lady and then bodied himself. I can't take living around shit like that dog, I had to go."

Lea was playing with the gauze on her broken fingernails and then stopped when she heard him. The anger in her eyes revealed that she wanted to go off on dude, but I raised my hand signaling for her to chill.

"Yeah that nigga that bodied himself was my pops. Watch ya' mouth homey, don't be speaking about shit you don't know." I said in a calm yet firm demeanor.

He held up both of his hands. "Oh nah, no disrespect, I just seen it on the news, I apologize. I ain't trying to be out of line at all dog." He sympathized, before picking the needle back up to start carving into my skin.

When he started, I heard the needle buzzing, yet I couldn't even feel the pain. I was numb and my mind was adrift, reveling with thoughts of my pops. I wrestled with holding back my tears, I wasn't the crying type of nigga but losing my pops hurt like shit. Flash backs of him placing the gun to his temple kept replaying in my mind and his voice continued to echo, "Take care of your sister." And on my life, I felt like I was losing my mind.

"Alright my dude, you're done." He finished my tattoo so fast, I didn't even realize that I was bleeding.

He wiped the blood away and told me to take a look at my new tat. I sat up and looked in the full-length mirror at my father's face on my chest and I almost started bawling. His skills were on point, my tattoo looked identical to the picture I gave him. "You good, is it straight?" He asked me.

"Yeah it's cool, patch me up." I told him. He applied some clear gel and placed a clear plastic film over my tat. I raised up and Lea traded places with me preparing for her turn. As he was sketching Lea's rose design, about three Cape Verdean dudes and one Spanish nigga wearing all black entered the shop to see him.

"Que paso' Pablo?" The Spanish dude began verbalizing to Pablo. I noticed that I knew one of the niggas in the pack; it was this cat Chino who I used to buy my weed from. I lost contact with him a few months ago because he was constantly switching up his numbers to avoid the jakes catching up to him.

"What's up Ant?" He greeted, gripping my arm tight.

"Ain't shit man, what's good with you?"

"Same ole' shit.'" He smiled.

He nodded his head to the tattoo artist. "Pablo, I hope you took care of my man, this is my people's right here." He told him.

"No doubt, I just hooked him up."

Chino scoped out my tat and winked, "Dope shit." He said to Pablo. Then he looked at me. "Call me Ant, got some good numbers for you."

"I ain't got ya' math no more man." I told him as I stretched my shirt back on.

"A'ight, get it from Pablo, make sure you hit me though." He instructed.

"I got you." I told him.

Pablo led the pack to the back of the shop and told Lea to give him a few minutes and he'll get back to her.

I picked up a magazine off the crowded counter top and browsed through it. Lamborghini's and Rolls Royce's filled the pages and I tossed it back on the counter because it reminded me of pops. He loved cars, although he couldn't afford them. It was always a dream of his to floss in something luxurious. He would always say, "An old man can dream, right?"

Lea and I sat there for a good ten minutes waiting for Pablo. She was squirming in the tattoo chair, growing more impatient by the minute. She kept patting her legs and rolling her eyes. "Man he needs to hurry up, I ain't trying to be up in here all day." She barked.

I curiously raised my head toward the back door that they disappeared into. Being a hood nigga, I knew what they were doing in that back room. Clearly Pablo was copping some work. That nigga Chino was the man, he was known for getting bread. He always stayed dipped up and driving something smooth. I had to give it up to Pablo and respect his hustle. The nigga was running a tat shop and obviously hustling out of the shop as well, he was clearly about his money.

Finally they returned into the common area. "Hasta Luego." Pablo waved them off as the pack exited out of the front door.

Before Chino could leave, he nodded my way, "Hit me up Ant." Then he lifted his head up to Pablo again. "Pablo, don't charge them, that's my people's, a'ight?"

Pablo nodded. "A'ight, they are good then."

Once Pablo was done with Lea's tattoo, he told me that since Chino co-signed for me, we didn't have to pay. That's how good I had it in my hood. Chino respected me because I never shorted him and was always good on my word. With pops so heavy on my mind, I forgot to get Chino's number before we left.

When we got home, I checked the messages on our house phone. There was a message from the coroner's office asking what we wanted to do with pop's body. I felt like a piece of shit because I didn't have enough money to bury my own father. Funeral's ran anywhere from five grand and up. I didn't have five grand and even if I did, I would need it to hold the household down. I made a hasty decision to have him cremated because there was no way that I could afford a funeral with only a G to my name.

With a heavy heart, I called the coroner's office back and informed them that they could cremate him that same day. Shit hurt a nigga to the core to have to have my pops go out like this, but I had no choice. I had to sit with feeling like I had let pops *and* Lea down. Mentally and emotionally, I had hit an all-time low. Slowly I hung up the phone and was left with an overwhelming emptiness burning in the pit of my stomach. That's when I realized that I hadn't eaten all day, my appetite had been non-existent because of all the stress.

I opened the fridge to find only eggs, butter and some old noodles pops was eating from last week. I slammed the fridge shut in frustration. My back was up against the wall and I was now responsible for rent, food, Lea, and all the bills. The little nickel and diming I was doing was not going to help us any.

41

"Yo Lea, call one of your girls and ask if we could buy like a hunnet worth of food stamps!" I pitched.

"A'ight!" she yelled back from her bedroom.

Slumping down at the kitchen table, I forced myself to come up with something to get us out of this hole we were in but I couldn't come up with shit. In pure frustration, I was about to knock everything off the table when I noticed the white envelope that my mom's husband Larry left on the table. Slowly, I peeled it open and discovered that it included twenty-five hundred dollars inside. With my eyes wide open, I shuffled the money in my hand and began to strategize. Fuck the bullshit, it was time to make some real money and I had a plan.

Chapter 3

I made my way back to the tattoo shop the next day. Pablo greeted me as if he had known me for years.

"What's up Ant?" He asked enthusiastically in his Spanish accent.

"Ain't shit." I said. I saw him stretch on a latex glove as he prepped for his next customer at his booth. The familiar beauty was a girl that I went to school with named Nicky. From the looks of the stencil, she appeared to only be getting three small hearts which she asked him to place in the back of her ear. I told Pablo that I'd wait for him to finish her up to holla' at him.

I squat in one of the chairs in the waiting area. I picked up an XXL magazine off the glass shelf, pretending to go through it. I falsely scanned through the pages but instead of paying attention to the content, I was actually thinking about Nicky. She looked good as shit! She had that intoxicating beauty. In high school, she was all skin and bones but it looked like she had picked up some weight. She was half Puerto Rican, half black, long brown straight hair and a straight TEN! She wasn't too thick, she had that tear drop ass and a small waist. Her facial features exuded that exotic look like Lauren London but she had that hood swag like Nicki Minaj.

Nicky knew she looked good, she was confident and from what I heard, she kept her head in the books after high school. Most of the girls I knew from around the way didn't attend college, but Nicky went to Northeastern University and she carried herself, with style and grace, yet she was hood at the same time. The combination attracted me, heavy! She was every hood nigga's dream girl.

After finishing up shading in the last heart of her tattoo pattern, Pablo handed Nicky a square mirror to look at the back of her ear in the big mirror. "Yes I love it Papi!" She smiled in approval and kissed Pablo on the cheek, wiping off the pink lipstick she smeared on it.

"You ain't charging me right cuz?" She asked pointing at him with her long red fingernail.

He smiled and slid off his gloves. "You good lil' cuz, call me later." He winked.

Nicky picked up her purse and before she left, she smiled at me and said, "Hey Ant." Then she walked out. I tossed the magazine to the side and tried to catch her outside.

"Yo' Nick?"

She spun around. "Yeeesss?" She sang out.

"You still stay on Harvard Street?" I asked.

"Nah, I moved. I live on Glenway now." She answered.

"Well, put my math in your phone; let me take you out."

She smiled. "You're trouble Ant, I stay away from trouble."

"I ain't trouble, I promise." I said with my hands up. "Let me take you out, we need to catch up." I insisted.

She reached in her purse for her iphone X and handed it to me. "Okay go ahead and put your number in my phone." She suggested.

Before I entered my digits, I noticed her titties were smiling at me through her low cut orange top, her shits didn't seem that big in high school but right now they were supple and sat up at attention. I did some thirsty nigga shit and sent myself a quick text from her phone so that I also had her number.

She playfully tapped my shoulder and smirked. "Sending yourself a text, huh? That was some real slick shit Ant." She laughed and saved my number into her contacts.

"I'm a slick nigga." I teased, on my smooth shit.

She giggled, "I'll call you soon." I watched as she walked off, strutting in her six inch stilettos and white tight jeans with the cut outs in the front. She was sexy as fuck, she made a nigga's dick stand up strong.

"Make sure you do." I licked my lips.

Nicky kind of reminded me of my sister Lea but Nicky was more into her education. She was a pharmacist Manager employed at the Plaza at the pharmacy around the way. She and I used to kick it back in the day, nothing serious, I never hit it or nothing but shorty was just real cool to kick it with. I remembered her as being real easy to talk to.

I snapped out of that mushy shit and made my way back into the shop.

"Damn, it's a small world, you know my cousin Nicky?" Pablo asked me while cleaning off his booth.

"Yeah, we went to school together and shit."

"That's what's up. She's a good girl." He said.

Suddenly a tall dark-skinned dude ran into the shop. "Yo' Pablo, you leaving for the day, can you ink me up real quick?" He asked.

"Nah, just finished the last tat for today my dude, I'm closing early today. Come back in the morning, I'm going to open the shop around ten.

"A'iight, I got you." The dude peeped over at me, "Oh what up Ant? I didn't see you over there my nigga. What's good?"

"I'm chilling, what's good with you?" I greeted. "Same shit different toilet. You got some trees?" He asked me in a lower tone.

"Nah homey, nothing on me right now." I tapped my pockets.

"A'ight then my G, I'll hit you up."

"A'ight." I dismissed him.

"Damn you're the man around here, huh?" Pablo asked as he began locking up the shop.

"Nah I'm just me." I said.

He pulled down the curtains on the huge windows and unplugged the OPEN sign. "Have you spoke to Chino?" He asked me.

"Nah." I said.

Pablo smiled. "Well I heard you're *that dude* around your way, Chino put me on to how you handle shit and I respect it. He told me you're good people and trust me, Chino just don't look out for anybody dog. If you're good with him, you're good with me."

"That's what's up." I smirked. I was glad that he and I were on the same page. I had come into his shop to talk business and Pablo was hip to it. The shit was so perfect. Real recognize real and I had met up with Pablo at the perfect time. Pablo picked up a broom that was leaning against the wall by his tattoo chair and he swept under his booth. Soon after we smoked a jay and kicked it for a little while. Turns out, we knew a lot of the same people.

Pablo was a hustler too and hustlers were usually strategic. It made sense that we did business together because the area where I lived was an untapped market for his crew and I was the key to getting them plugged in there.

Pablo exhaled and passed me the blunt. "Shit, since you live in Warren Gardens, I don't have any connects out your way, I usually deal with niggas in Revere and shit. I moved out of that neighborhood because shit was hot, if niggas around there knew what I was moving, I would have gotten robbed early." He nodded.

He now had me curious, I wanted to know what he was moving; I needed to be put on ASAP, I know it was risky but I wanted in.

I rubbed my hands together, "well nigga that's perfect, I can set up shop in the hood and move shit all day. You need a nigga like me on deck."

At first it seemed like he was pondering on my suggestion, and then he put out the blunt and motioned for me to follow him. He led me into the back room and clicked on the lights. The room was full of old black leather tattoo chairs and dusty tattoo books.

"No offense to you but I don't know you that well homey." He lifted up his shirt to reveal that he had a nine on his waist. It was his way of showing me that if I was trying to rob him, he had something for me. I put my hands up and smiled, "I respect it homey, I'm just tryna' eat."

He laughed it off and gave me dap. "Honestly I'm a good judge of character, I could tell you're a real nigga."

"No doubt." I said convincingly.

He picked up the same briefcase I saw the Cape Verdean dudes and Chino come into his shop with and opened it up. Thousands of small pills and a powder substance in small baggies were inside.

"What the fuck is this shit?" I asked.

"This is *my* weight homey. Less risky, easy to smuggle in and it's GOOD money."

"Damn." I said shaking my head staring at all the small white pills that filled the briefcase. "I ain't got no clientele for this my nigga."

He smiled. "Yo', these are perk 30's, ecstasy pills, Xanax, Oxy's, Vicodin and some more shit. The white powder is molly. You live in the hood, them fiends you see around, they don't just be on that white, trust me, perk 30's and Oxy's move all day. And I know you know some hood rats my nigga; them ecstasy pills and mollies move like water."

Pablo had a point and I realized the nigga was right. I know niggas that popped pills but I never thought about selling them. This nigga Pablo was on to something. I figured that this was going to be a challenge for me but I was convinced I could move anything in my hood. And like he said, this was less risky. The lower the risk, the better, Lea needed me out here.

Pablo counted over one hundred pills and placed them in a large ziplock bag. "I'm gonna let you hold something, you move it, bring me back my doe and we'll continue to break bread."

When I took the bag out of his hand, I knew it was time for me to show and prove. If this shit moved as easy as he said it did, I was about to be the man in my hood. Getting on Chino's good side would be beneficial and I knew that Pablo would put in a good word for me when it was all said and done. I concealed the pills in an old gym bag I had in my car and I went to the hood and got busy.

Chapter 4

I swear a nigga felt like Big Meech because all that shit he gave me went in two days. I shocked the shit out of Pablo when I showed up to the shop with his money. The smile on his face stretched from ear to ear. His expression was priceless.

"I told you this shit moves!" He was excited! He shut down the shop and led me to the back room. He tried to hand me my cut but I told him to keep it and just pay me in pills. I also gave him the entire twenty-five hunnet that my mom's husband left us. If I was gonna' hustle, I was hustling foreal! I didn't have time to nickel and dime, I needed real work so that I could come up fast, and that's exactly what I did.

I continued to move shit so quickly, my clientele tripled and my new burn-out phone, which wasn't linked to my name, was only used for business purposes and it stayed blowing up. Within a month, Pablo started giving me the full briefcase of pills to move and I had them shits pushed out on the streets so fast, I was surprising myself. I was all in, I had no idea that I could move pills like they were keys of coke and make all of this money. Pablo put me on to something that I was about to create an empire with but I needed a team of people that I trusted with me.

I planned on meeting up with the crew because it was time to expand my hustle and I needed people that I trusted in this with me. Plus I was making so much money, I wanted us all to eat together; them niggas was my family.

I pulled up to Terror's crib, I knew nigga's would be out on the porch shooting the shit, none of them niggas had jobs. I parked and then ran up on J-Boy. "Nigga give my sister Lea back her jeans, nigga." I

49

couldn't hold back on clowning his skinny ass girly looking jeans. Nigga was standing off the porch looking like Lil Wayne and shit. His dreads were fucked up but his outfit was clean. Terror and Leon also threw out some jokes about his jeans and his crew-neck shirt. I squat down on the porch to kick it with niggas.

"Yeah a'ight, y'all niggas need to step your swag up. Bitches don't like niggas with them baggy ass jeans and hoodies no more. Y'all stay on that Boston shit, Adidas and Timberlands, three's and trees. Niggas ain't seventeen no more dog. I rock this grown man shit." He popped his collar.

"Nigga I can take your girl with these baggy jeans on nigga." Leon jokingly ran down the stairs to buck up to J-Boy.

J-Boy stood up. "Man, the day I see y'all niggas pull a bitch like my girl Samantha is the day I'll salute y'all. Them hood rats y'all be pulling look like you can smell their pussy through their jeans."

"Ha, ha, you got jokes nigga, Amber looks way better than Samantha." Leon said confidently, stepping up closer into J-Boy's face.

"Nigga, Amber is sloppy and ugly as shit, that bitch don't look better than nobody." J-boy laughed.

They continued to go at each other's neck and as usual, I had to break it up because they always got serious after a while. They acted like brothers. One minute they were ride or die for each other, the next, they were at each other's necks. I peered around at all my homies. Here we were on the porch clowning on each other's clothes and who had the badder bitches when I was making all this money and basically had the power to change all of our lives. It was time for me to put my homies on. I felt comfortable enough with my hustle to set up a fool proof operation. I wouldn't have it any other way, breaking bread with my homies was a must.

"I heard you bagged bad ass Nicky?" Terror asked me, nodding his head in approval.

I smiled. "Yeah something like that."

J-Boy faced Terror and Leon. "Yo', why this nigga always gotta' act so humble? Niggas can't even hate, that's a bad bitch! Shit, you lucky I didn't catch up to her first, I would've bagged her. I wanted Nicky for years." He joked.

"Yeah, yeah, yeah. I bet you did. But yo', let's go to my crib real quick, I gotta' show y'all something." I stood off the porch and changed the subject. I was excited to show my team what my new hustle was. I didn't have time to be talking about bitches when there was so much money to get and I needed them to start thinking the same.

"I hope you got a bitch over there for me." J-Boy joked.

I nodded and smiled. "Nah, I got something better."

Everyone squeezed into my car and I aimed to the crib. Once inside, Terror rolled a blunt and J-Boy was hollaring about calling some bitches to come through. Leon's crazy ass was just sitting back chilling, who knows what was going on in that crazy nigga's mind.

I stood in front of my homies like I was a teacher in a classroom about to give a lecture. The thoughts racing through my head had me excited. I planned to take over my neighborhood and the money we were going to make would be substantial if all went well. Before I could get a word out, we heard a loud commotion coming from outside my front door.

"Who the fuck is that?" J-boy raised off the couch toward the window as we heard the yelling heightening. The loudest voice I heard was my sister's. Once I heard Donte's name being mentioned, I knew it was some female drama. I opened the front door and aimed toward the

51

porch. Lea was yelling loud and being dramatic with her hands at the top of the porch.

"Y'all hoes just make money for him, he don't want none of y'all broke down bitches so stay in your lane. Y'all wish Donte wanted y'all dusty hoes. Just make money for him and don't worry about our relationship because I ain't going nowhere!"

"Yeah whatever bitch!" A pitch from some loud mouth ugly bitch with a yellow scarf on yelled from the pack of five girls at the bottom of the stairs. From the looks of their attire; short miniskirts and clear high heels, clearly they were Donte's hoes. This nigga was supposed to be pimping hoes and having my sister as a girlfriend and the shit didn't make sense. Pimps didn't have girlfriends, that nigga was just a lame nigga getting money off dumb, lost bitches. It seemed as if his hoes were mad because he was fucking all of them and they were jealous that my sister wasn't making money for him but got treated with more respect than he had for them. Well if you call the dumb treatment my sister was getting from him respect.

"Lea get your ass in the house!" I snatched her up. Her little crazy ass would've jumped off the porch and tried to fight all five of them broke down thots if I hadn't came outside. She was crazy like that, but I wasn't about to let my sister fight over no lame ass nigga.

"Y'all need to make a hair appointment with me to get your hair done because y'all look broke the fuck down! Recognize who you're dealing with! Y'all bitches better google me!" Lea shouted as I forced her inside.

"Get your ass in here talking about google you, they won't find shit. Shut UP!" I handed Lea's dramatic ass over to J-Boy and told him to hold her. I went back on the porch to put a stop to this dumb shit.

"Ay! Yo', y'all hoes better get the fuck from in front of my crib before I have my sister smack the shit outta' all of y'all one-by-one."

"Yeah whatever, tell her to stay away from our daddy Donte. Tired of her ass!" The loud chick pronounced. She nodded to the rest of the hoes and rolled her eyes. I could tell she was probably his bottom bitch because they followed her lead. "Let's go y'all." She snapped around and the ugly hoes followed her.

Leon stepped on the front porch and looked at me with a serious look on his face. "You want me to rob all of them Ant?" He asked.

"Man, you get the fuck in the house too, what's wrong with y'all? I don't need no hot shit going on at the crib."

"I'm just saying." Leon said. His crazy ass was always ready to get into some shit.

Finally we were all inside and I sealed the door shut and locked it.

"See this is what I'm talking about, hot shit like this can't happen!" I barked. You could probably see the steam coming out of my ears. "Now I need y'all to shut the fuck up and listen!"

My homies were looking at me wondering where all the aggression was coming from. I was sonning everyone like they were my kids but I was on to something and I needed our crew to be tight knit. I stormed into my bedroom and retrieved a Timberland boot box full of money. I slammed it on the coffee table and opened the box. I had five thick stacks of cash in large rubber bands.

"What the fuck!" Terror blurted out in shock.

"Who's money is that bro?" Lea asked taking a seat at the edge of the couch.

53

"It's mine." I stated firmly.

Everyone sat puzzled with eager eyes, awaiting an explanation for all the cash that was in front of them.

"I got a new hustle." I revealed with pride. I picked up one of stacks and waved it in front of them. "Obviously it's been pretty lucrative. If I have y'all on board, we could kill em'". I preached confidently.

Terror stood up. "Dog, I thought you said you didn't want to sell white when I told you about my Dominican connect, how you gonna' go cop some weight behind my back when I told you I wanted in?"

"Nigga sit down!" I demanded. "This doe ain't from pushing white." My words knocked him back on the couch. I had everyone's full attention.

"This is what I push." I finally revealed one of the bags of pills from my jean pocket.

"Medicine, nigga?" Leon asked as he took the bag out of my hand to examine it.

"Leon, dog just shut the fuck up and listen man, y'all niggas talk too much!" I snapped. "Now listen. My man put me on, I be getting off all types of shit, P-30's, Xanax, Vicodin, Oxy's, Opiates, and I got E pills and mollies too. I've been out here making a killin'! At first I figured I didn't have no clientele for it but I been out here doing my thing. We could kill em' out here y'all. I get the pills for ten dollar or less each and sell them for $25 and up all day."

"Twenty five dollars for one pill?" Lea asked with curious eyes.

"Twenty five dollars for one pill." I repeated in her face.

"Shit I'm down, I know I could get anything off out here." J-boy said confidently sitting up on the couch.

"That's what I'm talking about." I said appreciative of his initiative. "If I would've known that I would make all this money selling these pills, I woulda' held off on letting them cremate my pops. Do y'all know how I feel as a man to not have had enough money to bury my own pops?"

Lea put her head down and everyone shook their heads and sympathized. We all sat in silence for a moment. I think we were all reflecting in our thoughts.

"One thing my pops always preached was to break bread with your family." I gave everyone a serious look. "And y'all are my family." I grabbed another one of the stacks from the table and held it up. "In pop's honor, I want y'all each to take one of these stacks." The stacks were divided into ten racks in separate rubber bands. Everyone grabbed their stacks, pulled off the rubber band and sorted through the money seeming stunned at the amount. Niggas couldn't believe my generosity.

I smiled because it felt good to see my team eat.

"I made 50g's already and being the real nigga that I am, I just gave all of y'all ten racks each which only leaves me with ten too. That's how dedicated I am to this team. We have to look out for each other. The money is going to get better but we can't have no loose links. Y'all never been the type to pop pills and shit so I ain't worried about y'all using the supply. But once shit pops, no extreme flossing, no bird bitches knowing what y'all do unless they are customers and no getting greedy. And don't serve no customers where you live, do everything away from where you lay your head. Now, I just showed my true colors, I had 50 racks to my name and just basically gave it to y'all. I want y'all to show me the same respect in return by staying loyal."

Terror looked like he was almost in tears. He stood up to give me dap. "Damn. That's some real nigga shit. I'm all in my G." J-Boy stood up next. "Shit I'm in too. This ten racks alone is a come up."

Leon was still seated and he hadn't lifted his head.

"Yo Leon? Leon? You in?" J-boy asked him.

Finally he faced our direction with a serious look on his face. "Oh my fault, I couldn't hear y'all, I was busy counting money over hea' NIGGA!!" He flung hundreds into the air and we all burst out laughing! Leon never seen ten racks in his life. Us getting any kind of money was saving a nigga like Leon's life. He did too much crazy shit and he needed to be slowed down.

He raised himself off the couch and dapped me up strong. "This is some real shit Ant. I owe you my nigga, I owe you my life." He looked in my eyes, "I would do anything for you." From the look on his face, I knew that he meant every word. "You hear me? Anything, my nigga." He said again.

"Trust me, I know Leon. Now let's get this money."

Chapter 5

My crew got busy, literally! I schooled them on the pricing of the pills and J-boy and Terror came back that same night needing to re-up. Leon took a little longer but he was getting off a lot of the pills on the streets too. It all seemed too easy and honestly we were moving too fast. After two months, we moved 30k pills which translated to seven hundred and fifty thousand dollars. The hood was officiallyn ours! We were so discreet about our shit that you wouldn't be able to trace it back to us if you wanted to. Pablo on the other hand wasn't so lucky. His tattoo shop was raided and he was arrested on site. The news of his arrest really shocked me because it made me aware of the risks that I was taking. Making the type of money that he was making out of a tattoo shop was hot in the first place, but who was I to tell a nigga how he should hustle. Chino had also got caught up because he and Pablo did a lot of their business by phone and their lines were being recorded. Although I had a burn out phone, I had purposely never even had one conversation with Pablo by phone regarding business just in case some shit like this happened, I dealt with him and Chino in person only.

Since Chino wasn't just pushing pills, the nigga had weed and massive quantities of cocaine in his possession also, his operation was hot and he got smoked by the judge! I promised myself that I wouldn't be that greedy and I stuck to what I was doing, pills only! My operation was so lucrative and so easy, I had to be smart about shit. Thankfully Chino had just introduced me to his connects and I had begun dealing with them directly.

The connects fucked with me because they knew I was official. My operation had now expanded beyond my hood. I had Lea and her girls driving from Boston to Miami once every two weeks to pick up packages. I bought a navy blue 2000 Honda Civic just for that purpose.

The custom-made-stash was cut into the seam of the seats so they were good if they got pulled over. There was no way po-po would find anything in that whip. I hated putting my sister at risk but I couldn't trust anyone else to make the drive and I needed Terror, J-boy and Leon in the hood moving shit. I knew that Lea wouldn't tell her girls what she was making the trip for, she was too loyal to the team for that. Plus them bitches never been out the hood before, so driving to Miami was something that they wouldn't refuse and Lea needed the company on the road.

One day, Lea had returned from one of her Miami trips and I had surprised her with her first Gucci bag, diamond necklace and matching earrings. The biggest surprise that day was when I pulled up to the dealership and told her to pick out any whip she wanted. She cried like shit! We never could afford no shit like that and she was just in awe at the fact that the empire I was building was really more for her benefit than anything or anyone else.

"Bro, this is crazy. It's like this is all too good to be true man." Tears gathered at her eyes.

"I know." I agreed. "But I told you I was going to take care of you. That's what pops wanted, so that's what I'm gonna' do. I want you to save all the money I give you, use it towards College or something beneficial for your future. I'll take care of everything else."

"Man, you are dope bro. I swear you are." Her eyes smiled at me. She bent into a black Lexus and circled her hands around the leather steering wheel. I figured that she'd be okay to floss in something new. To the jakes, she'd look like a woman who works an honest job and got herself a new Lexus. For myself, I was staying in my hoopdie till I felt safe enough to upgrade.

I followed behind Lea as she drove her new car home. My baby sister thought she was the shit with her music blasting through the hood for everyone to see her but I loved every minute of it. The rapper Young Thug's screechy voice sounded out through her speakers, *I done did a lot of shit just to live this here lifestyle!*

Ironically we rolled by Donte's hoes that came to my crib with all that drama that day. They were strutting down Blue Hill Avenue and Lea didn't miss a chance to show out. She slowed down and beeped her horn. "What's up you dusty, broke, raggedy ass bitches!!! Haaaaa!" She turned the music all the way up and skid off. I couldn't do anything but laugh. Although she was sassy as fuck, watching my sister shine, gave me the greatest joy.

When we got home, Lea embraced me with the strongest hug ever. Simultaneously our focus went on a family picture of me, her and pops that sat on our old TV. Pops was smiling mad hard in the picture. "I miss him Ant, I miss daddy so much." She said sadly.

"Me too." I whispered.

I noticed tears drawing out of Lea's eyes. "Pops loved that old ass TV." She chuckled through her tears walking toward it. "Let's go furniture shopping Ant, let's get all new shit. There's too many memories here." She said.

I nodded. "I agree baby sis."

She picked up the picture and took a deep breath. "Promise me one thing Ant? We have to keep this TV as a keepsake, fuck it, we'll just buy a flat screen to put on top of it."

I laughed, "A'ight cool." I agreed and then I nodded again. "Damn, pops got that shit in the 80's and never upgraded it." I huffed and Lea released more chuckles about the TV through her tears.

"Pops was a cool ass dude man." I began channeling memories of him. I truly wished he was alive to enjoy some of the perks of our new foundation.

"He's still with us Ant, I know he is. He's with us in here." Lea put her finger to my heart.

"You already know." I said. I peeled out five grand from my pocket and gave it to Lea to get new furnishings for the crib and to get some shit for herself.

My phone began ringing and I kept ignoring it until I felt that my sister was okay. I hated to see her crying. She was my priority and her happiness came before anything, even work. She wiped her tears and I sat beside her on the couch. She tilted her head on my shoulder and eventually began nodding off but the noise from my ringing phone kept waking her up.

"Bro, you can go, I'm okay." She insisted. "I'm gonna' take a nap because I have to do someone's hair later."

"You sure sis?" I asked her.

"Yes, Ant, I'm okay, I promise. Go handle your business." She assured me stretching out on the other side of the couch to go to sleep.

I kissed her on the cheek and admired her as she sank into a deep slumber. All I wanted to do was make sure she was okay and go hard out in the streets for her. "I'll see you in a bit sis."

I screened my missed calls, slid into my whip and read a text message from J-Boy. He asked me to come to his crib to talk business. I was about to tell him to meet me somewhere else to kick it because I tried to avoid going to his crib ever since pops died. I knew his mom wanted to know how I was dealing with everything, but I harbored a grudge against her ever since my mom said that she told her about

60

pop's death. If she was able to get in touch with my mom after all these years that easily, why the fuck didn't she ever give me and Lea her contact information? I was really hoping that she wouldn't be home, but when I got there, she answered the door.

"Is J-Boy here?" I asked, knowing he was inside.

Looking just like the Actress Loretta Devine, she opened the door to let me in. "Give me a hug Ant." She put out her cigarette in the square ashtray on the kitchen table and squeezed me tight. Although I didn't want to feel her embrace, it felt so warm and genuine since she was the closest thing I've ever had to a mom. "I been so worried about you and Lea child, you have no idea." She tried making eye contact but I refused.

"I'm okay. I'm good." I told her.

My Aunt stood in front of me trying to sear her eyes into mine but I refused to give her eye contact.

Letting out a huff, she squat down and lit another cigarette. "Did you see your mom?" She asked in a lower tone.

Her words crawled under my skin and she almost automatically forced me to tell her how I really felt. "Yeah I did. I heard you were the one who contacted her about pops." My tone was purposely aggressive.

She took a pull from her cigarette. "Yea, I did."

I nodded. "All these years and you knew how to get in touch with my mother? Why didn't you give me her information when I used to come over here crying when I was a youngin'? Why didn't you give us her information when you knew my sister needed a mother figure in her life?"

Flicking the ashes off the tip of her cigarette into the air, she smiled. "Why do you think I loved on y'all so hard? I tried to be that mother figure to y'all because I knew that she couldn't."

"What the FUCK you mean she couldn't? That shit don't make no sense!"

Raising up from her chair, she pointed in my face. "Now what you are NOT gonna' do, is disrespect my house Anthony Currington!"

"Shit, you disrespected me by sending that lady to my house!"

J-Boy ran into the kitchen. "What's going on in here?" He stood in between us with one hand up to both of our chests.

"The reason your mom left is too complicated for you to understand and I never felt like it was my place to tell you or Lea. Trust me, I tried everything to get her back into your lives. Your mom and dad's past is deep Anthony."

"Shit don't matter now! I'm a grown ass man and I don't need no mother. Fuck that lady! And since you know how to contact her, make sure you tell her that her son, Anthony Currington said, Ma, FUCK YOU!" I stuck my middle finger up and J-Boy forced me into his room which was just outside of the kitchen and slammed the door shut.

"Yo' what the fuck is all that shit about?" He snapped.

Squatting on his bed, I couldn't respond. I saw J-Boy in front of me talking but I couldn't hear him. The inside of my stomach was doing somersaults and my mind was numb. My mom was a subject that was often never talked about. It was one of those things that I tried to push into a shelve in the back of my mind in order to help me to forget her.

Against my will, tears fell freely down my face and I couldn't control them. All the hurt and pain I harbored against my mom were coming out. My entire life was fucked up because my mother wasn't around and now I was realizing it more than ever before. I was so jealous of anyone who had their mom present and all it did was make me resent my own mom and the only thing I could do was block those feelings out and keep it moving. Now J-boy's mom had the audacity to tell me that my mom couldn't be in my life because of some sort of distorted past. Shit didn't make sense!

"Dog, dog, you a'ight?" J-Boy kept trying to snap me out of my zone.

With tears stained on my face, I raised my head to my homey, "I miss my pops man. I just realized that besides Lea, I really have no family, my nigga. My life's fucked up!"

My words seemed to make J-Boy emotional too, I saw his eyes gloss up but he swiftly looked away from me. None of my homies had ever seen me express myself before. I was always the one keeping other motherfucker's from being sensitive, giving advice or breaking some shit up between the crew. But this was a real moment for me. If he wasn't like my family, I don't think I would've allowed myself to become this vulnerable.

"Listen Ant man, I'm your family nigga." He beat his chest with his fist. "Fuck blood, I still consider myself your cousin *and* pops my uncle! I miss him too bro. We doing our thing out here Ant; pops would be proud of how you for holding shit down for Lea."

Standing up from the bed, I paced the room. My mind was all over the place. It was on Lea, my mom and my pops. I had the weight of the world on my shoulders.

"You hear me my nigga?" J-Boy was still trying to calm me down.

I stopped in my tracks because his voice had finally became clear. "I hear you dog. I gotta' stay focused man, all this shit and especially this shit with my pop, keep fuckin' me up."

"Well I'm here my nigga'. Blood, sweat and tears, we all we got, let's not let this be the end of pop's story."

"Yeah, you're right. That's real." I said. J-Boy dapped me up with a hug. I really needed this time to finally mourn some of the pain and aggression I was feeling and in a way; it felt good.

Once I got myself together, I peeped all the new clothes on J-Boy's bed. This nigga was finally able to purchase authentic gear and throw out all that bootleg shit he used to rock. I saw boxes with silver and gold Prada, Versace and Giuseppe sneakers. And of course in regular Boston fashion, he had a variety of Adidas and Timberland boots.

Laid across his dresser were every color skinny leg jeans and top hats to go with them. This nigga stayed sporting the most extreme and bizarre shit. I even saw different color bow ties.

"I see you went shopping nigga, damn. What you buy the whole mall?"

"Shit, you know I gotta' stay on for the bitches. Plus I think when it's all said and done, I may use my doe to open up a store in Nebraska or some shit. Show them niggas out there how to dress." He rubbed his hands together while admiring his own collection.

"That's what I'm talking about. Just stay doing it how you're doing it my nigga. Don't buy no over the top car or no new house and shit, continue to stay low key. Stack all your doe and open up not just one, but multiple stores my nigga. Gotta' have goals so big that it makes you feel uncomfortable. I'm glad your mind is right."

"I'm hip." He said, then he pointed to the bag that I was carrying. "You got that for me?" He asked.

I handed him the bag of supplies and then collected some money that he had for me and I got myself together to leave.

I walked by my Aunt who was still sitting in the same kitchen chair smoking before I left. I couldn't bring myself to apologize to her because I was still angry. I didn't understand what all the secret shit was about. If my mom's and pop's history ran deep, then she needed to tell me about it or keep that shit to herself. If it was that serious, I knew sooner or later, it would be revealed.

Chapter 6

My trap phone didn't stop ringing daily and it gave me an adrenaline rush just knowing how much money was out on the streets to be made. My personal phone was only used for Lea and the crew. We spoke in codes and made sure most business was only discussed in person.

As I was heading to one of my stops, I noticed an unfamiliar number calling my personal phone and I almost didn't answer it.

"What up, who this?" I answered.
A petite chuckle resounded through the speaker. "Hey Ant, it's Nicky, how are you?"

I felt like a lame because I couldn't help the smile that reached my face.

"Nicky, Nick! What it do baby girl?"

"Damn, you didn't save my number? I guess that's why you haven't reached out yet. You texted yourself from my phone and I saved it, so I thought you would have at least saved mine."

"Daaamn babe, calm down." I laughed. "You got me tho, I didn't have your shit saved but I'm gonna' save it right now."

Our laughs filled the speaker. "It's all good, what are you up to? We should catch up soon, I'd really like to see you." She said.

Nicky was aggressive and I liked it. She was confident and wasn't afraid to put herself out there.

"Shit, a nigga been busy but I can make time for you. Let's do movies or dinner or something soon."

"Nope. No dinner, no movies, how about we start off with you coming by tonight and we just sit in the car, listen to music and catch up? Or we can go for a walk around Franklin Park."

"Damn, we demanding huh?" I teased.

"Not demanding, just a little sterned." She laughed.

"Ha, ha, okay. You got it ma, we can definitely catch up. Let me free up some time and then I'll hit you up."

"Okay Papi, I look forward to it. Talk to you soon."

"A'ight."

"Wait Ant." She stopped me.

"What up?"

"Well I don't want to step on any toes. Do you have a girlfriend? I know you used to deal with a lot of little thotties back in school but I don't remember you ever having a serious girlfriend."

"Because I really never did and no, I don't have a girl now. We'll discuss all this when we link up, okay baby girl?"

"Okay Ant, talk to you soon." She said sweetly.

I hung up to answer my trap phone that was ringing hot. I made a few plays and then I met up with Leon at this small liquor store on Warren Street. He kept texting me some shit about him fucking up.

I parked my car in front of the Liquor store and bent to tie my shoe. When I stood to my feet, rolling in that bitch nigga Donte's Deville again was my little sister Lea, cruising up the street. It was the most smiling that I had seen her do since pops had died. She leaned over and kissed him on the cheek and then he made a turn onto a nearby street and the duo disappeared. Instantly, I went from zero to a hundred, I was HEATED!

I stormed into the liquor store.

"What's good my dude?" Leon greeted. He looked at me funny. "Damn, what's up with the ice grill nigga?" He asked, standing in front of the freezer full of malt liquor.

"Man, I just saw my sister with that nigga Donte again. I told her to leave that nigga the fuck alone! Her dumb ass don't listen man!" I pat my fist into my palm.

"What? She still fuckin' with him? I thought she deaded that shit."

"Yo she's gonna make me *dead* that nigga literally." I nodded and tried to manage my anger because I wanted to hop in my car and go find them. My sister knew better than that shit.

Leon wiped off his smirk and a serious look dominated his face. His slow steps toward me showed that he meant business. He whispered in my ear. "You want him deaded? Then you got that shit my nigga. You saved my life nigga, all this money is what's gonna' take me and the fam' out the hood for good. I'll do anything for you, just give me the word."

It was at that moment that I had forgot who I was venting to.

"Did you hear me, I said I would do anything for you, just give say GO!" He pat his waist with his hand to let me know he was strapped.

Leon would do anything for me if I put the battery in his back. If I gave him the word to handle Donte, he would! I swear every time Leon saw me, he spilled out how appreciative he was that we were family and how all this new money was changing his life, but I didn't need him out here doing anything crazy. We didn't need any heat like that around us, especially right now. So I knew I had to diffuse my delivery to keep him focused.

"Nah, I'm just poppin' shit nigga, I don't want to kill the nigga but I'm gonna' end up fuckin him up again. Nigga got my sister's head all fucked up, you know I don't play that shit dog. Lea is off limits."

"Yeah I know, Lea's like my little sister too. Don't let me catch that nigga sleeping or I'm gonna' get rid of that problem for you."

"Yeah whatever nigga." I turned my attention to the liquor store clerk. "Yo', let me get a pack of swishas and that 1738."

Leon twisted his back to the counter and faced the entrance while biting down on his bottom lip. Who knows what this nigga had calculating in his brain because he was always on some other shit. Little did I know, I would soon find out.

I paid for my shit and knocked him out of his trance.

"So what's up nigga, I got money out here to get, what was that shit you was texting me about?"

"Oh, you ain't gonna believe this shit I gotta' tell you my nigga." We hit the exit and posted up next to my car.

"What? What happened nigga? You acting like some crazy shit happened."

"Nigga some crazy shit *did* happen! Yo, Amber *and* Alicia is pregnant."

I laughed. "Get the fuck out of here!"

He tilt his head in my direction. "Man that shit ain't funny. I got two hoodrats pregnant, what kinda' shit is that?"

"Sounds like a personal problem my nigga." I laughed.

"Oh you got jokes today, right?"

"Nah' I'm fuckin with you but why the fuck wasn't you strappin up? That shit's your fault too."

"Man I hate condoms. I ain't gonna' front nigga, I never wear them shits!"

My smile broke. "Well then nigga you should've expected this then. Why ain't you wrapping up knowing these hoodrat bitches ain't loyal? You see what the fuck happened to my pops!"

"I know. That's what I need you here for my nigga."

"You need me here for what?

"To help me ask these hoes to get abortions."

I started cracking up. "Nigga you ain't serious right?"

The serious look on Leon's face as he paused in front of me was undeniable.

"I'm dead serious. What should I do nigga?" He asked me.

I peeked over both of my shoulders and then pointed to myself. "You asking *me* what you should do? I ain't got no seeds dog." I laughed.

"See you still think this shit is funny."

"Alright look my nigga, you just gonna' have to swallow this shit. You probably need this. You got two babies on the way, it's time for you to hang up all that crazy shit you be doing up. Once we make enough to get out of here for good, you need an exit plan. You gotta' invest your money into something that will keep you wealthy. You're about to bring two kids in this world so shits about to get real for you. You gotta' man up and handle your responsibilities. Nuff said."

"So should I get a new crib and move them both in?" He asked me.

I laughed again because he was clueless. "Listen nigga, just put yourself in a position to be prepared for when your seeds come. Getting this money should be a priority for you now."

"Oh it is, I'm getting so much money, I don't know what to do with it right now. I'm itching to splurge."

I nodded. "Nah, no splurging. Just stack up and do right by your seeds."

"Yeah you right. I love you dog, I'm about to go make these runs. Gotta' get this money, right?"

"That's what I'm talking about." I said.

"I'll see you later my nigga."

"A'ight dog." I said, before we parted ways.

I laughed about Leon's forever crazy ass antics as I hit the crib. Lea was unlocking the front door as I approached it.

"What up big bro?"

"Man. Don't what up me." I smirked.

"Daaamnnn!!! What the fuck is wrong with you? Why you acting stank in the middle of the day?" She opened the door and we both walked inside.

"I saw you with that nigga Donte' again."

"Ooooooh BOY!" She rolled her eyes and threw her purse on the couch.

"You think this shit is funny Lea? Why you ain't tryna' fuck with a nigga in College or a Corporate nigga? Why is my little sister fucking with a pimp? You are better than that yo'!"

"You can't help who you fall in love with Ant."

"Love? You don't love that nigga! So you loving my enemies now? You're my sister, your loyalty lies with the family, fuck is wrong with you?"

"Ant, he's good to me. He loves me and he makes me happy. One day we are probably going to get married."

I laughed. "So you wanna' marry a pimp? You sound dumb as shit! Not my little motherfuckin' sister. Fuck that!"

"So does the profession make the man?" She asked.

"Hell yeah!" I barked.

"So what does your job say about you then Ant?" Her sassy ass crossed her arms against her chest awaiting an answer.

As I was about to dig into my sister's ass, Nicky rang into my phone. I picked it up but had to finish barking at Lea before I answered it. "Yo', you heard me Lea, just stay the fuck away from that nigga, tired of telling you that shit."

"I heard you Ant, damn! Okay! I'll leave him alone if that makes you fuckin' happy!"

"It ends today!"

"I said okay!" She snapped.

I answered my phone and headed back out the front door.

"What up Nick?"

"Hey did you forget about me?" She asked. Her voice was so sweet and calming.

"Nah, I didn't forget about you baby girl."

"Well, what are you up to?" She asked.

"Ain't shit, bouta' hit these streets."

"Well I'd still like to see you today if possible."

"Yeah, that's cool. I'm going to make a few runs real quick and then I'll come through there. Text me your address."

"Cool, I look forward to it." She was enthralled, I could tell she was talking through a smile.

I hit a few corners and got some pills off. The money helped me forget about my spat with my sister and I looked forward to seeing Nicky. I sent her a text to let her know that I was on my way. When I hit Talbot Ave, an old skinny crack-head was selling flowers at a stop light and I purchased a bouquet of red roses for Nicky. I parked in front of her crib and sent another text to let her know that I was outside.

Her confident walk to the car in her low-cut stone wash jeans, red top that cut off under her perfect titties leaving the bottom half of her flat stomach showing, had a nigga's dick on rock. She was dope as fuck! She had that mesmerizing beauty.

73

Slowly she squat into the passenger seat and reached over for a hug. Her coconut smelling perfume beamed off her body as she squeezed tight and kissed me on the cheek. "Heeey Ant."

"Hey beautiful." I reached into the back seat to grab the flowers.

She palmed both of her cheeks and widened her mouth. "Ooooh my goodness, you got me flowers! Thank you Anthony." She licked her lips. "Let me find out you're a gentlemen." She said.

"Something like that." I flirted, placing them into her hands.

Tightening her eyes, she inhaled the scent of the flowers and then looked at them as if she was admiring them.

"You a'ight ma? You good?" I asked.

"Yeah I'm okay." She smiled my way. "I just love romance, I love when a man gives me chocolates and flowers, especially roses. White roses are my favorite. I think white roses signify innocence and purity. Like love in the highest form."

"Damn, you be getting deep with this romance shit. All this shit is new to me. Shit you're the first girl I got flowers for." I admitted, feeling like a fuck boy. I was the smash and go type nigga, never even wanted to spend a dime on a woman if her name wasn't Lea. Something about Nicky was different and I respected her. She was one of the only chicks I knew from the hood that went to College, had a job and didn't let many niggas from around the way smash. She was hood, yet classy, she didn't have a trash mouth and use 'nigga', 'dog' or 'motherfucka' behind her sentences like most of Lea's homegirls did.

74

"So you sure you don't want to hit a bar or go grab something to eat?" I asked.

She nodded. "Nope, I'm a simple girl. I just want to sit here and kick it with you. Haven't talked to you or seen you in years."

"Damn, we can't even go inside your crib to talk?" I pushed again.

Her pretty face turned serious. "Come on Ant, I'm not just gonna' invite you into my house, this is the first time we chilled in like forever. Continue being a gentlemen tonight. Okay?"

I chuckled. "Okay ma, you got that."

"So what's up Ant, what's new?" She asked.

"Nothing much, same shit."

"I heard about your dad, I'm sorry." She bowed her head down to her lap and nodded.

"Thanks. So what's up with you, you still working at the Plaza at the Pharmacy? Do you like what you do?" I changed the subject.

"Yes, I'm still working there. I like what I do a lot, but writing is my passion. It may sound corny but I'm a die-hard poetry head. I feel like poetry allows us a chance to use our words to express ourselves and share it with the world. I'm actually working on a poetry book."

"Word? That's what's up."

Nicky went on to talk to me about her future endeavors, how she wanted to eventually move out of the hood and how she was sick of all of the violence in Boston. Although normally I wouldn't want to hear this shit, I was intrigued because she brought something different to the table. She wasn't just talking about Gucci bags and the latest shoes coming out. She had substance, so in turn, I spent the rest of the night catching up with her and then agreed to scoop her for lunch at her job to have our official first date. But before the night ended, I was meeting up with the homies at the club. We had made so much money that week, we agreed to celebrate and since we'd been keeping shit low and didn't do too much shining; we were using this night to do it BIG!

Chapter 7

I admired myself in the mirror before I left the crib. The fresh line-up around my Caesar was on point. Finally I was able to slip out of my grinding gear and rock some of the Giovanni shit that I purchased from Saks. A nigga was fresh and fuckin' clean stepping into the club. I was on my pretty boy, J-Boy shit. My black jeans weren't too baggy and not too fitted and the Golden G in my Giovanni shirt made the golden spikes on my black Loubs kill the fuckin game! We purchased two sections in the club, one for our crew and one for Lea and her hood ass girls. All eyes were on us because we ordered fifty bottles of Rose Moet, twenty bottles of Ace of Spades and invited all the pretty bitches and real niggas in the club to party with us.

"Let's fuck up some commas, let's fuck up some commas yea!!!" Terror screamed out the lyrics to the rapper Future's song as the DJ pointed to our section. "We got some real niggas in the building, Ant and his crew are in here fuckin' up commas!" The club cheered us on like we were celebrities and I really didn't like all the attention. I loved my city but when niggas knew you were getting more money than them in Boston, robbing you was something you should probably expect to see coming. We had all the baddest bitches in our section and all the real niggas were saluting us for showing love.

Looking around at everyone admiring me, I realized just how much power I had. I was getting so much money, I was the fuckin' man! When I was younger I used to look up to the hustlers, now all the hustlers I used to look up to were in our section looking up to me. The hood and the game was ours. I took a good look at my niggas and everyone looked like they just smelled like money. Niggas was shining foreal! Our lives were changing and we deserved it.

I cracked the fuck up as drunk ass Leon held two bottles in his hands the entire night double fisting and getting fucked up. Peeking into the crowd, I noticed some niggas mean mugging us as they walked by our section admiring our bottles. One in particular looked like the rapper Fat Joe and he particularly kept his eye on me. "Fuck that nigga lookin' at?" Terror asked.

"Fuck him!" I retorted.

"Hope we don't have to pop the trunk on niggas tonight!"

"Fuck that hating ass nigga. Turn up!" I said. Conveniently the DJ switched the music to Future's song, *"God's Blessing all the trap niggas."* Our entire section turned up! Lea and her girl's started twerking on the couches and doing all types of ratchet shit. The bitch nigga that was scoping us out had disappeared into the crowd and we continued to enjoy the night.

Cautiously watching my back as we hit the parking lot, I dismissed my homies and searched for Lea to ride home with me. I spotted her and her ratchet crew by the entrance. She was checking her phone and smiling.

"Okay y'all, I'm out. I loveeee my bitchesss!!! We turned the FUCK up tonight girls!" Lea hollared as she blew kisses to her girls and them mud-ducks turned around and twerked her way before heading to their cars.

"Haaa! I swear I love y'all hoes. I'll see y'all later." She said. Suddenly Donte's car pulled up and Lea disappeared inside. I was too fucked up to cause a scene so I watched as my sister drove away with my enemy whom she just told me she wasn't gonna' fuck with anymore.

I was fucked up but somehow I managed to make it home. I always parked away from the crib but close enough to peep the entrance. Looking toward my porch, I spotted a gang of black hooded niggas running up and balancing themselves off the porch into the main entrance. I sobered up quick as shit! There were other petty drug dealers living in my complex but I was almost certain that they were heading to my apartment. I hit up Terror first because burners were something I knew he had on deck and I told him to meet me at my crib with a *sweater*, which was code for bring the heat. He let the crew know what was up and within minutes they were parked behind me.

Terror leveled himself into my passenger seat with the crew popping in the back seat and they asked me what was up. I pointed to the last nigga that tip-toed up the stairs and my niggas knew automatically what time it was. I could still smell the liquor on everyone but niggas were alert and ready for whatever. All except for Leon's drunk ass. He was drunk and belligerent and was almost appearing more than just drunk. I'd hoped he wasn't using none of his supply.

"Man let's go and kill all them niggas. Let's kill them all execution style, I don't give a fuck! Niggas tryna' get up in my nigga Ant's crib, they all just signed their death certificates!"

"Shhh! Yo' chill out Leon man. You're drunk dog. Stay your ass in the car." I demanded.

"Let's kill them niggas and post their bodies on Instagram." He chuckled.

"Nigga I told you to delete that Instagram shit, you better not be posting pictures of money and shit on there either, you're gonna' make us hot!"

He started laughing. "M-o-n-e-y is the password to the Instagram page. Our page is lit, niggas need to see how we live! Haaa!"

"Yo', now's not the time for all that. Nigga just shut up and stay your drunk ass the fuck in the car!"

He laid his head back on the seat and closed his eyes. He was in no condition for a mission. The rest of us quickly hatched a plan to catch them niggas when they came out. Thankfully I never kept no work or no money at the crib, so they would automatically come up short.

Terror popped his trunk and pulled out some big, dumb-stupid shit. These guns were so big, I didn't even know if I'd be able to work the shit but my game face was on and I took mine off safety.

We ran up to the area of where they parked and waited. The dumb ass niggas thought that they parked their car in the cut but it was to our advantage. It was perfect enough for us to hide in some bushes and not be seen by anyone on the street, or by them when they came out.

We exchanged intense glances and J-Boy cocked his gun back. "We brothers! Nothing comes between the family. Let's rock these niggas to sleep." He whispered and smirked.

Suddenly we heard running steps toward their cars.

"Come on niggas, let's go! He wasn't there and there wasn't shit in there!" One of them whispered out. All three of them niggas ran to their separate doors, opened it and squat inside. Silently, me, Terror and J-boy ran up on them before they could shut the door. I made sure that I ran up on the driver because most likely he was the leader of the pack. Simultaneously our guns were pointed in their faces.

"Oh y'all niggas thought y'all were coming up, huh?" I forced the driver's black hood off his head and instantly I recognized him as the Fat Joe looking nigga that was ice grilling us in the club a little while ago.

"Oh you're the hating ass nigga from earlier." BOOM! I hit him in the head with the back of my gun and made him run everything in his pockets. Blood dripped out of his mouth and nose and I think I even saw a few of his front teeth fall out. J-Boy and Terror robbed the nigga in the passenger and backseat and took their guns. "Let this be a lesson, you can't fuck with real niggas! If I ever see y'all around here again, it's your HEAD!" I hit the nigga over the head with the gun again making sure that he felt my wrath.

"Let's go!" I commanded to J-Boy and Terror. J-Boy still had his gun up to the nigga's head. "We just gonna' let them go? Let's kill these niggas Ant." He was anxious.

I locked eyes with him. "I said come on nigga." I demanded.

We shut the door and ran off. "I'll see you again Ant. This shit is personal nigga." The driver hollared as he started the car and sped off.

We made sure they cleared the street before we hit my car.

"Why didn't we kill them Ant?" J-Boy asked as we sat inside. He was dramatic and turnt up!

"Y'all didn't kill them niggas?" Leon's drunk ass woke up talking out his ass.

"Yo', we in this for money, not no reputation, we ain't catching bodies out here man! Use your head!"

"But Ant, these niggas tried to rob you! They would've probably kidnapped you if you were home. What the fuck! We should've killed them niggas! Now they out here and we gotta' watch our backs!"

"But they *didn't* kill me nigga! Be smart J! You ain't no killer, you want to make this money and leave the hood or you wanna' make money and get locked up and trapped in the hood for life?"

Stifling our argument, Terror started laughing. "Fuck is so funny?" J-Boy
barked.

"Them niggas tried to rob us and we ended up robbing them."
He sorted through all the guns we had just stolen from them. "More shit
to add to my collection." He laughed.

"Man shut up." J-Boy spat. He was still mad that we didn't body
them niggas and he left the car angry. I followed him and Terror to their
cribs to make sure they were good. I dropped drunk as Leon off at his
crib after because he was in no condition to drive. As a unit, we had to
make sure we were all safe. I headed to a hotel and stayed the night
there. I knew Lea was probably staying with that nigga Donte but I text
her and told her that I didn't want her at the crib anymore because it
was hot. Memories of pops and me and Lea growing up will forever live
in our old apartment, but it was time for us to move.

As I laid my head to sleep that night, I couldn't get that Fat Joe
looking nigga out of my head. He said that it was personal. I couldn't
help but to wonder if he was one of Donte's boys, or one of Trisha's
sons trying to get even for my pops killing her or just some stick-up kids.
Whoever it was, I was more than sure that I'd see them again.

Chapter 8

Immediately I rented a condo. We finally had our own dwelling in Randolph under Lea's name. I couldn't be too far out of the hood because I had to be able to get there and then be able to pop right back home when needed. I switched up my car and purchased another modest whip, a black 2001 Acura. I didn't want nothing too stupid to get our white neighbors curious to pry into our business.

Since Lea never used the money I gave her to redecorate our old spot, I had told her to just bank it. But now that we were in our new crib, I figured that making the crib feel more at home was something we could do as a family because I really didn't see my little sister much unless it was about business. I missed her and wanted to spend more time with her. Her ass was too busy running the streets and sneaking off to be with that nigga Donte thinking I didn't know.

I hired some Mexicans to move our shit. All we took were our clothes and pop's old TV. Everything else we could do without, well that's what Lea kept saying. The longer we held on to all the memories, the harder it was for us to move on. She was happy about our new spot. We lived amongst white people and no one knew us in our area. I just wanted my sister to feel safe and to continue making enough money to move out of Boston altogether.

It didn't take long for us to hook up the new spot. Everything was in it's proper place and all of the furniture and fixtures that Lea picked out accommodated the space graciously.

"We did good bro." Lea admired the plush white couches, turquoise accent pillows and the white marble coffee and end tables. "There's just one more thing to make our house a home." She reached into her large Celine bag and took out our family picture and placed it in the center of the coffee table. "Now this is home." She smiled. I kissed my sister on the cheek and then answered my ringing phone.

"Yo. What up?"

"Hey Papi, you all moved into your new spot?" Nicky asked.

"Yeah man, finally. A nigga is tired."

"Aww. Well do you feel like grabbing some lunch? My treat. I'm taking a late lunch in about an hour, I'd love to see you."

I glanced at all the missed calls on my trap phone and decided to answer them later. I made sure Lea didn't need me to move any more furniture around and I headed out to meet Nicky. Seeing her was always like a breath of fresh air and a nigga needed some air.

I parked in front of Nicky's job and texted her when I was outside. I had on my brown Ray Ban Aviator lenses while I was laid back in my seat with some trap music turned all the way up. When I saw Nicky walking out of the building, I sat up in my seat to get a full glimpse. She unzipped her white pharmacy jacket as she was approaching my car and it was like things were moving in slow motion. Not only did the black dress underneath her smock hug her thick hips and accentuate her breasts but an idea clicked in my head that I couldn't believe I hadn't thought of. Nicky was the plug and she didn't even know it! She worked at a fuckin' pharmacy which stayed pumping with clients all day and I needed that. Instead of just trying to hang with her and possibly hit it, I needed to earn Nicky's trust and see if she was loyal.

I took her out to lunch at this spot on Newbury Street but I couldn't stop thinking about the possibilities of her being able to expand my clientele. I knew I had to see where her mind was at, and that's what I planned on doing.

After a few more lunch dates, two months quickly blasted by us. Nicky and I were still seeing each other quite often and my crew was still moving shit like a transportation company. We hadn't seen any of them niggas that tried to rob my crib and our game was now tighter than ever. The entire ordeal made us closer as a unit and we were more like a family than ever before. Every night we'd call each other to see if everyone was good before we laid our head down.

Any down time that I had, was either spent with my sister Lea or with Nicky after hours. It was obvious that Nicky was beginning to fall for a nigga because every time I took her out, she would gaze into my eyes when we weren't talking. Then she started with the pet names and shit like 'boo' or 'baby' and I just rolled with it. I can't front, I enjoyed her company and her conversation. It was just really easy to be with her. She never really complained about petty shit like most females, she was just focused on making a nigga happy. In the past, I never felt the need to give a female too much of my time but I found myself wanting to kick it with her more and more. She was like one of my niggas but just sexy as fuck! She was becoming a part of my life and it was time to put her to the test, I wanted her to meet Lea.

I invited her over to the crib and Lea was excited to meet her. But of course in true Lea fashion, she had to pop some shit before she got there.

"She better be pretty too." Lea sassed, hopping up on the kitchen island.

"Oh you got jokes? She's prettier than all your hoodrat ass friends." I teased her.

"All my friends are pretty, I don't know what you're talking about." She defended.

"Laura is the only friend you have that's pretty, all your other friends act and look like niggas." I joked.

She threw the roll of paper towels toward my head. I laughed and dodged it and then we heard the doorbell rang.

"That must be Nicky." Lea hopped off the island and sped toward the door.

"Damn, calm down." I said following behind her.

Lea widened the door. "You must be Nicky." She greeted.

Nicky walked inside. "Yes, I'm Nicky, you must be Lea." She said confidently, while reaching her hand out to shake Lea's hand.

Lea looked over at me. "Daaaamn! You got a professional one, she's shaking hands and shit. Nicky laughed and then reached her arms out. "Actually, I'd prefer a hug." She squeezed Lea tight and then walked my way.

"Hi baby." She pecked my lips.

"Baby?" Lea repeated loudly. "Y'all got pet names now? Daaamn! This is real Ant!"

I laughed. "Chill Lea, you doing too much."

"No, she's fine Ant. I love her personality." Nicky smiled.

"Yaaaas! I like her already." Lea said batting her eyes and snapping her fingers. She took Nicky's compliment to the head.

Nicky looked around at our newly furnished crib. "This is really nice, you guys have great taste." She complimented before bending down to look at the picture of me, Lea and pops on the coffee table. "So this must be your father who you are always talking about. He looks like he was a great man." She said admiring the picture.

Lea stepped closer to me and whispered. "Ant, I really like her. Her vibe is genuine. Don't mess this up." She said.

I was truly surprised. Lea didn't like anyone, so the fact that she took a liking to Nicky right away placed the stamp of approval on our situation.

Lea's opinion meant a lot to me and I was glad that she took to Nicky's dopeness. The vibe was literally genuine and Nicky stayed over all night watching movies and drinking henny with me and Lea. It was the perfect break that I needed from the outside world. I welcomed the temporary escape and staring at the two women who were special to me smiling and vibing in good spirits was what a nigga needed.

Nicky headed out to the store later that night and returned with some Spanish food to cook. Shit, me and Lea hadn't cooked in our kitchen since we moved in that bitch. But Nicky put it to great use and Lea kept winking at me the entire time to give me her approval of Nicky. Especially after she tasted Nicky's food, she kept throwing compliments at her. I can't front, that pollo rice and beans was the truth. Nicky was the total package.

After we finished eating, Nicky kissed my lips and I walked her to her car.

"Your sister is dope." She said.

"Well she thinks you're dope too, which is rare, she doesn't like nobody." I told her.

She smiled and just stared at me.

"Why you all in a niggas face?" I joked.

"I don't see a nigga, I see a man who a lot of people have love for. Your sister definitely loves you. The bond you two share, you don't see often. You love her hard, and it's genuine. Hopefully one day I can have your heart too. You are amazing Anthony." She said.

Her words made a nigga uncomfortable. Talking about feelings and shit wasn't my thing. My mom had my head fucked up when it came to trusting girls, shit, I guess a nigga had abandonment issues because of my mother but how could you blame me?

"I'll call you later." I said kissing her again before seeing her off.

After that day, all I found myself doing was thinking about Nicky. We spoke every night, she made sure that her voice was the last voice I heard before I fell asleep. I tried to keep my head in the game and stay focused on what I needed from her but on this particular day, we had caught a movie and after, she finally invited me inside her crib. While she was in the shower, I ran down to the corner of the street to purchase a bouquet of red roses from another crack-head. Nicky was all about that romantic shit and I knew that the roses would earn a nigga some brownie points. I sat my back against her tall mahogany headboard with one foot bent on the bed and one of the floor. I felt like a bitch holding the roses in my lap but when she returned to the bedroom dressed in a red towel around her damp body and drying her curly hair with a small white towel, my dick went brick.

"Aww baby, you got me some flowers again?" She tossed the small white towel on her dresser, retrieved the flowers from my lap and kissed my lips slowly.

Taking in the scent of the roses, she squeezed her eyes shut and smiled. Once she opened her eyes, she paused. "Ant, you know I love roses and I feel really special right now, but baby I told you that white roses were my favorite. You have to listen when a woman tells you what she likes."

"Damn, I'm sorry love. Shit, I just thought flowers were flowers."

Her smile broke. "Nevermind Ant." She tossed the bouquet on her dresser and traded it for the small white towel to finish drying her hair. Then she turned around to finish talking shit. "You know I take this romantic shit seriously Ant. White roses are pure, it represents the purest form of love. Call me corny but I'm just in love with love."

Standing off the bed, I pulled her close to me. "I'm sorry ma, I promise I'll get it right next time, okay?" A brief pause halted the atmosphere. "Okay?" I repeated, gazing into her eyes.

Not able to resist my charm, a smile snuck back on her face. "Okay." She said softly.

I forwarded her body closer to mine and when she felt my dick on her thigh, she twitched.

"What's wrong Nick?" I asked seductively. I pushed her body even closer so she could get a better feel of my fully erect dick.

She smiled. "Nothing's wrong Ant, everything is right."

Removing her towel and dropping it to the floor, she pushed me down on the bed and her aggression was turning me on.

"I just want to please you Papi." She said.

The view in front of me had me excited; I was gonna' tear that ass up. Her hour glass shape could be compared to Draya's from the show, *Basketball Wives* yet her Puerto Rican side gave her hips and ass more curve. I was anxious to get knee deep into that pussy. She yanked off my sneakers and forced down my sweat pants. "You ready for me Papi?" She asked crawling toward me on the bed.

"Hell yeah." I said. My dick was on rock, I was ready.

"Mmmmm." She moaned as she took all of my dick into her mouth like a pro. "Ahh, ahh, ay!" She moaned, choking and slurping back on my dick. It was as if she was spilling out Puerto Rican melodies as she sucked it. I don't know what the fuck she was doing differently but her head game was on another level. It was sloppy, wet and perfect. She slid my dick out of her mouth and then she stuck it in between her fat titties and started spitting on it. Every time my dick hit her chin, she would suck it. Her love faces were so sexy, I had to stay focused so that I wouldn't nut too soon. She was on some futuristic shit like she was purposely trying to get a nigga sprung.

"Let me get in that pussy now." I told her.

"Sure Papi. Come get in this pussy." She stuck her finger into her pussy, licked it slowly and then laid back. I was never the type of nigga to eat no pussy but I wanted to taste her badly. When I did, her moans echoed the room and I couldn't help but crave to enter that pussy. I sucked on her sweet pink clit until she came and then I reached on the floor for my sweatpants, took out a condom and I tore that pussy up. Her shit was so wet and so tight, I pulled out a few times just to stop myself from nutting fast.

"Damn this pussy is good."

"It's your good pussy Papi. I don't want no one else." She moaned, staring into my eyes as I stroked.

"You hear me Papi? It's yours." She repeated into my eyes.

I smiled at her beautiful face and then tilted my head up as I felt myself about to cum. "Shit, I'm about to cum baby."

"You bout' to cum Papi? Come on baby, I'm gonna' cum with you daddy. Oh, oh Ooooooh! Papiiii!!"

I jerked back and forth, my strokes increased in intensity and I exploded into the condom.

"Aaahhh!!" That nut felt so fuckin' good. Her pussy was incredible! She kept doing some shit with her pussy squeezing it tight on my dick and that shit was the truth! I don't know if this was the best sex that I ever had because of how sexually mature she was or because I was catching feelings. Whatever the case was, she had a nigga open.

I slid the condom off and placed it on the floor on top of the wrapper. Still panting, I laid back and submerged the back of my head into the pillow and faced the ceiling. Nicky bounced into the bathroom to clean herself off and returned to wipe my dick with a warm wash cloth. She laid her head on my chest and took her fingers and made small circles around my six pack.

"I'm really falling for you Ant. I don't usually fall this quick but you're different. You're a dope person, inside and out."

"You're dope too." I said. She lifted her head to look at my face. "I'm dope too? That's all?" She sat up and forced her back against the headboard and nodded.

I stayed in position, a nigga was tired and all this emotional shit wasn't what I wanted to hear after a nut.

"You can't go through life avoiding love Ant. Open up a little bit, love is the greatest emotion GOD blessed us with."

I put my arms behind my head and looked up at the ceiling. "I wish I could ma, but it's not that easy." I said honestly.

"Look Ant, I know what you've been through with your mom. But every woman is *not* like her! Everyone will not abandon you. I know that *I* won't, I promise. I just wish that you could believe in me. Believe in *us* and trust me."

I heard what she was saying but instead of absorbing the mushy shit, the word *trust* stuck out. Trusting a woman was something that was never in the cards for me. It scared me but I also knew that Nicky was different. I sat up in the bed next to her and pulled her close to me.

"Listen Nicky. I do like you, and trust me, just me saying those words is new to me. You really have been dope. You keep a nigga in line. I like talking to you at night because it calms me. I'm just out here trying to make sure everyone around me is good and you are my something different. And to be honest with you, yes, I do trust you."

She smiled. "You do?" She asked.

"No doubt. That's why I want to open up to you a little bit about what I do."

"I'm listening." She said, biting down on her supple bottom lip.

I briefed her slightly on my operation but I didn't get too deep because although I felt I could trust her, I didn't want her knowing too much.

"So where do I come in at?" She asked. Nicky almost made my dick hard again because she was a fuckin' ride or die bitch foreal!

"Well since you work at a pharmacy, all I need you to do is give my boy J-boy all the addresses of the client's that fill prescriptions for Vicodin, Oxy's and Perks and I'll give you a list of the rest. I wouldn't get you involved any deeper than that. I don't need you helping me with the supply, I have my own connects for that, I just want the new client info so that I can expand my clientele and make this money even faster and I'm good."

"Done! I'll compile a spreadsheet of all the clients with repeated prescriptions for those pills and label the categories with names and addresses beside them and have it for you by tomorrow." She smiled and placed a slow kiss on my lips. "I got your back Ant, I just hope you have mine."

I smiled back. "Damn, that's what I'm talking about."

"So what are you gonna' do with the list I give you?" She asked.

"Just let me handle that. I'm going to text you my cousin J-Boy's information tomorrow. I'll need you to give him the list and we'll handle how to get the clients. They are so addicted to this shit, them old heads will buy them from me in bulk."

"Alright Ant, I got it. Just know that I got your back, and I hope you have mine."

92

"You don't gotta' worry about shit no more, ever. I got you." I said, meaning every word I said.

She smiled and snuck in a French kiss before we went to bed. A nigga slept good that night, but I was anxious, I knew with my new little Trap Queen, Nicky, now on board, money was about to blow through the roof!

Chapter 9

J-Boy was on the job. He met up with Nicky after work the next day and she gave him a list of over 500 addresses. There was no stopping us, instead of hitting the pharmacy and having to get prescriptions from their doctors, the clients were able to buy shit off of us on the streets and we were about to kill em'!

I masked my feelings on selling the pills to the 70 and 80 year old women. I guess I figured that if they weren't getting them from us, they were gonna' get them from somewhere else. Word spread fast at an elderly living facility in Malden. Those old white folks didn't have shit else to spend their money on except for medication. Most of their rich kids abandoned them to live their own lives and all they did was pop pills. In turn, made us richer.

I didn't know how deep I wanted Nicky to be into this life because I didn't want her to get caught up in anything at the hands of me. But she had my back. Whenever any new customer would fill a prescription, even if they weren't repeated customers, she'd add them into the spreadsheet for me. We had unlimited clientele in no time. Money was coming in so fluently, nothing could stop my empire from becoming great. That was until, the money started getting to everyone's head and with money, came problems.

Leon had invited me to his crib. I made plans to see Nicky after I hooked up with him. His crazy ass got a new apartment in Dorchester and moved both Alicia and Amber into the crib. He told me they were cool with the fact that both of them were having his baby and I just had to see that shit for myself.

Leon's apartment was modest, he had one black leather couch and one suede black chair in the living room. The kitchen didn't even contain a microwave and wasn't shit in the refrigerator. In his bedroom was one mattress in the middle of wood floor, no dresser or nightstand. His clothes and Amber and Alicia's shit was just thrown in the closet, wasn't shit hung up. His appliances however, weren't so modest. This nigga had movie theater sized TVs in both his living room and bedroom that sat on it's own stand and he had a sound system that could be heard from another state.

I squat down on the suede chair in the living room looking around at all the empty space. His apartment was huge for no reason. "Yo' you did some nigga shit by getting these big ass TV's in every room but then have this small ass couch and an expensive mattress on the damn floor in your bedroom. Where's the rest of your furniture nigga? At least you could do is use some of that bread to hook your shit up."

"Nigga, I ain't no interior decorator, I don't know how to do this shit, that's their job." He pointed at Alicia and Amber who were sitting beside him on the couch looking like two obedient slaves. Leon took puffs from the blunt he rolled up and then passed it to the girls. Pregnant and all, they both took turns inhaling the weed and then tried passing it to me.

"Nah, I'm straight." I rejected the blunt. "Yo' Leon, why you got them in here smoking and shit while they're pregnant?"

"Man, I don't got them doing shit. They are grown ass women, they are gonna' do what they are gonna' do regardless."

"Nah, you can check that shit."

"Fuck all that." He said puffing on the blunt and waving them off.

Amber stood up. "You want something to eat Leon, I can go out and get something to cook?"

"No! Cause' your ass can't cook! Call Joe's and order me a steak and cheese sub. Alicia, go pick out some shit for me to wear, I'm going out later."

"You're going out again? You just went out last night." She pouted, rubbing her protruding belly.

"Don't worry about what the fuck I'm doing, just go pick out my shit!"

Both girls did what they were told and I shook my head. He had two mud-duck looking bitches with low self-esteem willing to accept the fact that they weren't the only woman. I had to give it to him, at least he was up front and willing to let them know what it is. The system seemed to be working for the trio and I'd hoped that it would slow his crazy ass down a little bit.

"Damn nigga, seems like you got shit locked over here."

"They know what it is." He said. I noticed his eyes were lower than usual and his pupils were dilated. It was more than obvious that it wasn't just the weed that was making him that way.

"Nigga I hope you ain't fuckin' with them pills."

He laughed. "Hell no, I'm just high as fuck!" He said. But I could tell otherwise.

Suddenly a text from Nicky flashed through my phone and it had a picture attached. Nicky's beautiful caramel body was butt ass naked, her nipples were calling me and her bare pussy was fiending for my dick. *Can't wait to see you papi*, is what the message read. I couldn't wait to see her, I was gonna' murder that box.

I took a few shots of henny with Leon and I told him that I was out.

"You ain't going out tonight?" He asked me.

"Nah, nigga, I'm laying low with Nick tonight."

He smiled. "Let me find out my nigga Ant is finally locked down."

"Never locked down my nigga."

"Yea a'ight. Well hit me up later my G." We dapped it up and I was out.

I arrived at Nicky's house within fifteen minutes. She answered the door wearing the same outfit she text me a picture of, her birthday suit. All that she had on was some red lipstick and red heels. I picked her up off her feet and headed to her room. She giggled, "I missed you so much today Ant."

"I missed you too." I told her as I tossed her sexy ass on the bed. She licked her lips and then curled her finger to motion for me to come near her. She crawled toward the end of the bed and when I bent down, she smacked me with a kiss. I stood tall and she slid her hands into my pants pockets and pulled out a bag of pills and one bag of powder. She held it at eye level and stared. "Have you ever tried any of these?" She asked me. "Hell no, I don't fuck with that shit, I just sell it."

"What's in these bags?" She asked me curiously holding them up to her eyes. "That's ecstasy and that's mollies. She stuck the ecstasy back into my pocket and then laid back on the bed opening the little bag that contained the molly. "I always hear rappers talking about this shit, I wanna' try it."

"Fucks no! You're too good for that shit, hell no!" I barked on her but it was too late. Nicky had sunk her tongue into the small baggy and closed her eyes to explore the experience. I ain't gonna' front, it made the freak in her go from a hunnet to a thousand that night and her pussy was so good, we eventually stopped using condoms.

After that day, I couldn't get the vision of Nicky sinking her tongue into the molly out of my head. She was too good for that shit! And although I enjoyed the intensity of the pleasure during sex, it wasn't worth her losing who she was for a quick boost. Not to mention, every time I saw her after that, it seemed like she was high and each time, she'd deny it. I even heard that her position at the Pharmacy was being questioned because she was coming in late constantly and she'd also began slacking on her school work. That's when I realized that I had now created a monster.

As for business, thanks to Nicky, our clientele in the hood was endless as well as in a few of the outskirts of Boston. South Boston is where I made the most money. It had a history of being a racist town so I had to move diligently in order to avoid the pigs. I now had a plan to take over Fall River as well. Fall River was an untapped market that was literally full of pill heads. I got in touch with the team and told them to meet me at a remote location by the water in Brockton to discuss the new plan. The location was riddled with trees and it had a single bench tucked in the cut. I rolled up through the rocky path and parked. I got out and waited on the bench for the crew to arrive. J-Boy and Terror showed up first, they both rolled together in J-boy's modest black 2000 Chrysler 300. Leon on the other hand drove up in a fuckin' brand new white Range Rover. Instantly I wanted to smack fire out that nigga.

"Turn your fuckin' music down nigga!" I stormed up to the driver's side.

Young Thug's song, *Got me a check, I gotta check!* Blasted even louder from the car when he rolled down the window. His smile was revealed and the custom diamond fronts with specs of gold on his bottom teeth had me even more turnt up! He cut off the car and the music.

"What's wrong with you my nigga?" I checked him. Then I scoped a Rolex on his right arm and a glowing pinky ring that still shined in the dark after he cut off his car lights.

Once he opened the door, I yanked on his Louis Vuitton shirt and forced him out of the car.

98

"Get off me nigga!" He snatched away from my grip. Luckily he did because I was about to hem him up to his truck.

Terror ran over to break up the commotion. "Yo' chill Ant, what's wrong with you?"

"Look at this nigga man! He came out this bitch driving a bright ass WHITE Range, flossing Rolex's and fronts and shit in his mouth, what the fuck are you doing nigga? You tryna' get us all jacked?"

"Man, I'm living, that's what I'm doing!" Leon barked back, seeming extra high on something.

J-Boy took a look at all of Leon's bling and seemed to be siding with him.

"Shit, I feel him Ant. I just bought this punk ass Chrysler to be low key but I want to floss too. I got too much money to be pretending to live average." I frowned in J-Boy's direction. I guess his designer clothes and shit wasn't enough, he was fiending to spend his money on other things too, but they had to be smart. The shit that we were doing was easy but the consequences that it came with it could be dire and niggas act like they were oblivious to that fact.

"Are you niggas serious? Don't y'all see the bigger picture? This ain't about us flossing out here for the streets to see, this is about our families being straight for life! Look what happened when them niggas tried to run up on my crib. Flossing will make more shit like that happen! We can do all that flossing shit later, right now we gotta' make sure our shit is tight. Starting with all of our operations. This shit is bigger than us man! Stop letting this money change how y'all see shit!"

The crew all looked at each other. It seemed as if they all knew deep down that I was right but we were hood niggas. Flossing was a way of showing that we had money and that we were doing better than any other nigga getting money. But I wanted my team to not just think inside the box and for the immediate. Stacking for the future and being low key was the only way we were going to be able to see longevity in this game.

Leon wiped the smug smurk off his face. "Alright, you right dog, you got it. I'll take the shit back and pawn all these jewels. Shit, I got two babies on the way, a nigga is stressed, I needed to do something to make me feel good." He popped the white collar on his shirt that I wrinkled and let out a sarcastic laugh. "Shit, I ain't gonna' front nigga, it felt good to floss around the hood and show these niggas who the fuck I am." He seared his eyes into mine. "But I'm with you boss man, I'll follow your lead. You got that."

"A'ight good." I schooled him.

Simultaneously, the crew and I approached the bench and I explained my plan to take over Fall River. As always, everyone was all in and listened with open ears. The crew left with their orders of operations and I headed back to the hood to handle business. I called to check on Lea, she told me that she wouldn't be home for a few days but had something important to tell me. She refused to tell me where she'd be staying at, so I just told her to be safe.

As I hit the hood, I wrestled with the decision to keep my cash in a safe under my sister's name or Nicky's name at a bank. But I didn't want anything tied back to me. One thing was for sure, I needed to keep my shit somewhere solid. Once I hit 1.5 mill, that's when I was giving up the game, creating a wealthy escape for Lea and leaving the hood for good. So every day I was going harder and I was almost at my goal.

Chapter 10

"Hey Anthony. I missed you Papi." Nicky sang out into my phone. Her angelic Spanish accent always made a nigga smile, no matter what I was doing.

"You didn't miss a nigga." I teased.

"Of course I did baby."

"You just missed this DICK!" I joked.

She giggled into the phone. "Shut up babe, stop being nasty. I wanna' see you."

I glanced down at my trap phone and it was ringing hot. "I got runs and shit to make ma, I can't just swing through there like that."

"Anthony, can you just put me first for once? Please!" She pled innocently. I hadn't seen Nicky in over a week because of all the new clients we had and because of the expansion to Fall River. Shit was poppin' out in these streets. The dollars were intoxicating and I was determined to reach my goal. I didn't mean to neglect Nick, we still spoke every night and I had to admit, I missed her too. Although my feelings were growing for her at a rapid pace, this relationship shit was still uncharted territory for me. I knew that my feelings for her was strong, but I made it mandatory to keep my head in the game because I had shit to accomplish.

I paused and realized that I had to grab the new sheet she had compiled for me. "Oh yeah, you got that new spreadsheet ready right?"

She sucked her teeth. "I do. But Ant, I don't want you to just come over here about business. You know I just love spending time with you babe. We don't have to do nothing special, come over, give me a kiss, tell me how your day is going and let me give you a massage."

I took one more look at my trap phone in the passenger seat and I decided not to answer it. "A'ight beautiful. I'll be there."

I couldn't resist Nicky's advances. I took a detour on Columbia Road and decided to go see her sexy ass. To my surprise, she had a hot plate of Spanish food waiting for me and some henny on the rocks. It was hard to fight it, but she made a nigga feel emotions that I've never felt. She was tapping into feelings that I didn't even think existed in me. I didn't even know how to describe what I was feeling but it felt right. Her energy was always positive and she was really down for a nigga.

I finished my plate and retreated to her bedroom and I laid across her bed. I knew I couldn't stay long because I had shit to handle, but Nick insisted on giving me a massage. She played an old Drake song on her phone, *Best I've ever had*, slipped off my shirt and began to bless me with a hot oil massage.

She spoke as she massaged the tense muscles in my neck and back. My eyes were closed and I was enjoying every stroke of her fingertips. The massage was everything I needed after all the stress I had on my back from hustling hard every day. Always having to watch my back and always being worried about my sister and my team. Nicky brought serenity into my life and I appreciated her for it, but putting my full trust in a woman was still not in my plans.

"So baby I was thinking. After I finish school, I want you to leave Boston with me. I mean, what's really keeping you here?" She applied more oil to her hands and massaged small circles into my back and shoulders.

"My sister mainly. When my pops died, he told me to take care of her, so I can't leave until I know she's good. I mean, I plan to move away soon anyway but not until I know her and my team are straight."

"And what about you, who's making sure you are straight Ant?" She asked.

"My damn self." I said confidently.

She wiped her hands with a towel, got up and turned off the music. "Why don't you let me in Anthony? You keep purposely shutting me out and fighting your feelings for me. Everyone else around you is living their own lives and you are the only one consumed with helping them. What about *your* happiness? Don't you see that what we are building here is rare baby, we are meant for each other? I already love you."

Her words triggered an unfamiliar emotion and I didn't know how to respond to it. "You love me? Why? Why do you love me Nicky? Why would you love a hustling ass, thug ass nigga from Bean Town with no family?" I chuckled. "You're funny as fuck." I deflected.

"It's not a joke Anthony, I'm serious. I really love you! Why wouldn't I? You have a great heart and you are a phenomenal man. Loyalty is embedded into your DNA and I haven't seen anyone love his sister the way you love and protect Lea. I don't care about what you do or the fact that you don't have a family. We will create our own family one day. You're my baby." She crawled back on the bed in front of me and locked eyes with mine. I literally saw the love she had for me beaming from her sad brown eyes. She was desperate to prove her love to me but she didn't understand that it wasn't that easy for a nigga like me to accept.

"Baby, we have that kiss you at a red light type of love. I've never met a man with a heart like yours Anthony. It's so big and it has so much love in it to give but you keep protecting it from the wrong person. I'm never giving up on you until you love me back. And when you do, that's when everything will make sense."

"Fuck that supposed to mean?" I asked. Her words seemed deep but I still didn't understand that shit. I had too much going on to indulge in sensitive shit, I had to reach my goal and not let anything get in the way.

"You'll see." She said.

"Yeah a'ight." I said getting comfortable in her bed and turning over to take a power nap. All that mushy talk had me emotionally exhausted and Nicky didn't force the issue. I appreciated her for understanding, but I also knew that she was yearning for me to expose an emotion that I didn't know how to expose. She laid down beside me on the bed rubbing her hand up and down my back as I drifted off to sleep.

It was about nine at night when I left from Nick's crib with the new spreadsheet. Before I left, I broke her off a healthy amount of cash for the sheet and even more because she fucked with me tough and I didn't want her to want for nothing. Since J-Boy and Terror were now setting up shop in Fall River, I stopped by Leon's spot to drop the sheet off to him. He hadn't finished with the last sheet I gave him and he had really been fuckin' up when it came to business lately. I parked my car and shook my head when I saw the White Range Rover parked in front of his crib that he still hadn't taken back.

"This nigga don't listen." I whispered to myself exiting the car.

My Adidas hit the steps and I gave three strong knocks on the wooden door. I repeated the knocks but I didn't get an answer. I jogged back off the porch to look up the street to see if he was fuckin' with one of the bitches on his street, but I didn't see anyone. Suddenly, short sounds were heard from the back of the house. I crept to my car to retrieve my gun that was tucked in my sunroof and I slowly made steps to the back. Although it was dark next to the shed, I could see the back of what looked like Leon's head. "Yo,..Yo, Leon?" I called out. He turned around quick and shouted, "Oh shit! He pulled up his pants and quickly tried to secure his belt back on.

"What kinda' fuck shit is this!!!" I hollared after seeing what he was doing.

Apparently he was getting his dick sucked by a NIGGA! The flamboyant nigga raised off his knees and wiped his mouth with his hands. The motherfucker had a purple and black bob hair style and long curled eye lashes like a bitch.

"Damn Lee. Call me later, I guess." The gay nigga said to Leon before running past me dramatically.

"Leon? Are you fuckin' serious my nigga?" I was shocked and my fuckin' stomach was in knots. I wanted to throw the fuck up!

"I'm-I'm sorry dog. I don't know what the fuck is wrong with me man." Tears gathered at his eyes as he pulled his black shirt over his belt buckle. He desperately dropped down to his knees to plead to me. "Please don't tell nobody about this shit man. Please." He begged.

I was violently unmoved, there were no words formed at my mouth, I was disgusted with my nigga. I've never even imagined seeing my nigga in this light. Not Leon, he was one of the craziest nigga's I knew.

"Yo' Ant dog. Ever since my mom told me my father was gay, my mind been fucked up all life my nigga." This was the first time I had saw Leon cry and the nigga was crying hard. He sunk his head down to the ground before he continued. "I remember when I was younger man, my father used to sneak niggas in the crib to fuck when my mom wasn't home. One day while my father was in the shower, one of them niggas touched me dog. Can you believe that shit? Ant, another nigga actually touched my dick when I was a youngin' and then told me to touch his. I been so confused ever since, my nigga. It fucked my head up and I never told nobody. When my mom divorced him and told me that my pops was gay, I used to wonder if I was gay too since that nigga had touched me. That's why I've always been so reckless. I'm all fucked up in the head Ant."

My nigga seemed so vulnerable and confused. I didn't know rather to feel bad for him or be mad at him but it was too much for me to handle at that very moment.

"Damn Leon man, I don't know what to say."

"Dog, I'm sorry. I been popping these fuckin' pills tryna' get my mind right but it's making me worse." He cried.

I had no other words to offer him, I just had to get the fuck outta' there and try to erase what I had just saw outta' my head. "Yo', I gotta' go man. I'll kick it with you about this shit later. I gotta' go." I swiftly aimed for my car and skid off the street. It was hard for me to harbor bad feelings about my nigga because I loved him, he was my family, and I felt bad for what he had just revealed to me, but that shit I just saw was crazy! I couldn't even concentrate or think clearly. I ran right to where I felt the most comfortable at, Nicky's crib.

She opened the door surprised that I had popped up. "What are you doing back here baby?" She asked. "I just needed to see you man, I had a fucked up night." I pushed my way in and went straight to her bedroom to lay back on her bed. "You okay?" She was genuinely concerned.

"No I'm not. I just saw some crazy shit." I revealed. She kissed my lips and laid beside me. "You wanna' talk about it?" She asked.

"Nah, I'm still in shock. I just need to lay here and think real quick."

"Okay baby. It's going to be alright, I promise. I'm going to jump in the shower real quick and maybe we can get out the house and grab a drink to get your mind right. Besides, I think I have some news that might cheer you up." She French kissed me allowing the strawberry flavor from her gum to settle into my mouth.

While she showered, I sat up and took a blunt and some weed out of my pocket. I needed to smoke something bad. I pulled out a book from Nicky's bookshelf to crack my blunt on and I couldn't help but notice the title of the book in my lap because the shit took me by surprise. Then I noticed there were three more books stacked on top of each other with similar titles. The titles were: *The Art of Goldigging, How to Get a Man to Trust You, Make him Love you First, And He Shall Spend* and *Get The Man First, Then Get His Money*.

"What the FUCK!" I said shuffling through the pages of each of the books. She had pages highlighted with a yellow marker and seemed to be really studying the books like it was homework.

"What's wrong baby?" Nicky entered the room wearing a white robe, and was brushing her wet hair into a ponytail.

"What kinda' shit is this Nick?" I waved one of the books in front of her. "You tryna' make a nigga fall for you so that you can get in my pockets? I thought you were different! Is that why you always spitting that romance shit and how you wanna' move away and shit? You was tryna' finesse a nigga so I could finance you, huh? FUCK YOU!"

"What? How dare you talk to me like that Ant? I was real from day one. I don't want your money, I was never in this for that and you know it!" She threw her brush at me and cried.

"Then what the fuck are these books for?" I knocked her entire bookshelf down.

"Ahhh!!!! Stop Ant!!!" She hollared a frightening cry. "I was doing research for my poetry book to teach women how not to act! I was hoping to talk to you tonight over dinner and cheer you up with my good news about my poetry book deal. I got an email from the Publishing Company shortly after you left earlier with the acceptance letter. Now that you wanna' act like this, FUCK YOU! I want you to get the fuck out of my house Ant! You are so selfish, you wouldn't know what real love was if it was standing right in front you. You are just making excuses not to love me back! I never want to see you again. Get out!"

"You don't gotta' tell me to get out. I'm already outta' here!" I grabbed my phone and aimed toward the front door with Nicky at my heels crying. When I opened the door, to my surprise J-Boy was on the porch about to knock.

Stirring with emotions, I turned to Nicky.

"What the fuck is he doing here?"

"It's not what you think Ant!" She cried with her hands on top of her head.

"So you fuckin' my nigga?"

"No!" She shouted. I turned to buck up to J-Boy. "What the fuck are you doing over here dog? You did tell niggas you always had a crush on her since High School! You been fuckin' my bitch?"

"Hell no dog! You know I ain't on no shit like that. Come on Ant!"

Nicky forced herself in between us, crying and explaining herself. "Ant, I've been hitting him up to supply me with E pills and mollies. I didn't want to get them from you because I didn't want you to judge me. There is nothing going on with me and J-Boy, I swear on my life! I'd never do anything to hurt you. But it seems like you don't give a fuck about hurting me!" Tears melted down her beautiful face but I didn't want to hear that bullshit.

"Fuck both of y'all!" I left them both on the porch with my middle finger up and headed to my car.

"Ant! Anthony, I love you! Stop fighting this! I know you love me too! Why do you keep shutting me out and making excuses not to love me back? You don't understand how much I'm hurting inside! I can't take it anymore Anthony! I just want to be happy!" I heard her crying and yelling out outside my car. But I was out.

I hibernated at the W Hotel downtown Boston for two days straight. I didn't want to talk to anyone or see anyone until I got my mind right. I didn't order room service nor did I drink any liquor while I was processing shit. The only thing I did was smoke weed and reflect. J-Boy and Leon blew up my phone more than anyone. The only texts I was responding to were Lea's. I let her know that I was okay and she reminded me that she had some news to tell me. Since I hadn't seen her in what seemed like over a month, I told her that I'd meet her at the crib and I checked out of the hotel. I turned on my trap phone when I was in my car and tons of missed calls from clients chimed through. I knew I was missing out on a lot of money and I had to get my head back in the game.

J-Boy kept blowing up my personal phone while I was driving home so I finally decided to answer it.

"Yo?" I answered.

"Yo' Ant, you okay my nigga? We been looking all over for you."

"I'm good." I said nonchalantly as I swerved through the crowded streets.

"Yo' dog, on my life I didn't do shit with Nicky. When she first hit me up, she told me that she wanted to purchase mollies and E pills for her girls but when I asked her why she wasn't buying them from you, she told me the truth, that she was buying them for herself. She started hitting me up regularly for that shit and honestly dog, she's using that shit a little bit too much. You might have to check her on it."

"I believe you my nigga. That shit don't even matter no more, it's bro's before hoes anyway. Fuck her!"

"Yeah I feel you, but she loves you though my nigga, she's different, she's good for you Ant. She's down. Pops would've approved of her." He said sincerely.

After listening to J-Boy, I honestly believed him. J-Boy never did no shit to cross me, he was truly like my family foreal, but I was done with Nicky. Just thinking about how she was trying to play me with all that gold digging shit had me hot all over again. I ended my conversation with J-Boy and turned up my music to call me down.

As I was cruising down Warren Street, I spotted my sister Lea hopping out of Donte's car that was parked on the street a few lights ahead of me. I had to sit up in my seat to make sure I was seeing shit right. Part of me knew that she was still fucking with him but she told me she was done with him for the hundredth time and I wanted to believe her. The way that I was feeling had me wanting to take out all of my aggression on Donte. I was tired of Lea lying to me and telling me that she had stopped messing with that nigga.

I watched as she leaned inside his parked Deville and blew him a kiss before she entered the popular nail salon called Crave. I could see Donte's homey get out the backseat and jump into the passenger seat. Out of nowhere a White Range Rover crept up behind them from a side street. Once I realized it was Leon, things quickly moved fast. I watched as Leon parked behind Donte's car and crept to the driver's side where Donte was starting his car. Leon was dressed in all black and I could see the evil grin on his face from where I was.

BOOM!!!! Leon shot Donte in the head at point-blank-range. He then started licking shots into Donte's friend in the passenger seat. The wounded passenger managed to get the door open and began running down the street for his life. Leon chased him a ways up the street licking multiple shots in his back before the dude finally fell flat. It all went so quickly, I was banging my hands on my steering wheel and beeping the horn, rushing the light to turn green so that I could make it up to Leon and have him hop in the car with me.

"Come on! Come on! What the fuck!" I said rushing the light, the shit was taking forever. I would have ran that shit if I didn't have a car in front of me and one in the back of me. Suddenly I heard sirens nearing. Leon seemed too far away from his car to get back to it and make a get-away before the cops arrived because the siren sounds were too close. I wanted to ram into the car in front of me to help my homey get away. I saw him run back to his car with his gun in his right hand. No sooner than he got to his driver's side door, the police had already rushed on the scene from a side street. I beeped my horn so that the car in front of me could get out of my way but it was an old lady who appeared to be too scared to drive ahead after witnessing the shootings too. That's when I made the decision to put my car in park, take my key out the ignition and head up to where they had my homey surrounded.

"DROP YOUR WEAPON!" The police shouted with their guns pointed at Leon.

Leon was walking in circles like he was confused and all the white residue around his mouth revealed that he was high. They had my nigga surrounded and there was no way out for him.

"I ain't going to jail!" He shouted.

"I REPEAT, drop your weapon!" The kneeling officer yelled out through the loud intercom near his police car.

"I HATE you pigs! I ain't dropping shit!" Leon shouted then he spat.

"Leon, put it down dog! I got you, I'll bail you out, put it down!" I hollered as I grew closer.

When Leon spotted me, he smiled and then let out a devilish laugh.

"See my nigga! I did this all for you. I laid that nigga out because I love you dog. We are brothers man! I'm sorry about what you seen the other day dog. I'm sorry!" He pointed to Donte's dead body. "You see the shit I would do for you? I told you that I'd kill for you and that I'd lay my own life down for you if I had to. Donte's gone, I took care of that problem for you. Do you forgive me for what you saw the other day now?"

I felt tears falling out of my eyes and I pat my chest. "I forgive you dog, just put the gun down. We'll get through this."

"Hahahaha! We are brothers man. You, me and the crew, we are family, but niggas will never look at me the same if they knew my secret."

"Nigga, fuck that shit, it ain't about that right now."

"Just know that I love you dog, I told you I was gonna' handle that nigga for you and I did. I love you forever, but it's over. I ain't going out like this, these pigs ain't killing me and I can't keep from running from who I am. I don't wanna' live like this anymore. I'll see you when you cross over my nigga. Love you my G." Tears of sadness conveyed at his eyes as he pressed the gun into his mouth.

"Nooooooo!!!! What about your kids on the way man, think about your seeds! They need you!" I shouted.

"They are better off without me." POP!!!!!!

Leon shot himself through the mouth and the bullet flung out of the back of his throat.

"Noooooo! Noooooooooooooo!" I shouted. I couldn't breathe! I literally lost my breath as my friend, my brother, my homey dropped down to his death. My heart was racing a million miles a minute. I put my fist to my mouth and tried to fight the tears. "Leon man, what the fuck!" I cried. I couldn't believe my homey just took himself out like that, right in front of me like pops did.

My heart was racing fast. I turned away because seeing him laid out was killing me and my tears were overflowing. I felt myself shaking and I was losing my breath. My nigga was gone and there was nothing that I could do about it. I continued huffing and taking in intense breaths. "Damn Leon, not my nigga. I can't do this shit again!" The cops rushed toward him and took the gun out of his hand.

Suddenly my trance was interrupted by my little sister's cries. She ran out of the nail shop over to Donte. She was screaming and crying asking him to wake up.

"Donteeeee!!!! Donte, no baby, wake up. Don't leave me baby!!! Noooo!!!" Tears filled her face.

Three police officers proactively held her back as her screams grew louder.

"Ma'am, step away from him." They instructed.

"Noooo! Leave me alone, leave me aloneeeeeeeee!!! Please wake up Donte, wake up babyyyy!! I need you. I can't lose anyone else, I can't handle it! Please Donte, I can't handle it! Noooo!" My little sister shouted toward his lifeless body. The sensitivity in her cries shook me up.

Rushing to her side, I was stopped by an officer and immediately hemmed up. "Let me go, that's my sister man, let me go!" I hollered.

"We need you away from the crime scene." The officer shouted in my face.

The officers were able to get Lea away from Donte's car and closer toward me. She looked at me with the saddest eyes and shook her head. The officer let me go and I tried to comfort my sister but she stepped back. "Don't come near me Anthony, this is all your fault! I know you told Leon to do this shit. I hate you for this! I HATE YOU!!!" She cried so loud, everyone on the street looked in our direction.

"Shh! Don't be saying no shit like that out loud. Of course I didn't have nothing to do with this shit man! On G's!"

"Yes you did, I know you did. You had your little goon do your dirty work for you, knowing how much I cared about Donte. How could you do this shit to me! This shit ain't fair! I loved him! And I know how much you hated him, but guess what, now I HATE YOU!" She sped away from me dramatically and I watched as she emerged down the street alone. I could still see and hear her crying and I decided against following her. Her words really slashed through my heart. They cut deeper than death. Every single word was fatal, especially the words, *I HATE YOU*. My sister never used that word and my name in the same sentence no matter how mad she got. As much as she knew how much I didn't care for that nigga Donte, she had to have known that I wouldn't had killed the nigga, nor did I give orders to Leon to have him killed.

It was obvious that it would be an uphill battle to get my sister's trust back and I was prepared to do whatever it took to make sure that she was okay.

118

Chapter 11

The Funeral

Everyone from the streets who was anybody, showed up to pay their respects at Leon's wake. I paid for all the funeral arrangements and also put some money in his grandmother's pockets even though I knew she had access to all of Leon's money. I still felt the need to contribute, especially since she'd be the one helping to raise his two babies on the way. I instructed the funeral caretakers to make sure Leon had a closed casket because I knew my nigga didn't want anyone viewing his body for the last time in the condition he died in. I got a picture blown up of me, Leon, J-Boy and Terror and had it on an easel next to his casket. We were all smiling in the picture and the brotherhood was obvious.

Still in shock, I didn't have any more tears to cry. I sat in the front pew with Leon's family and I kept staring at the picture of us. None of this was supposed to happen. I would give all the money back, all the hustling, the thrill and all of this shit back just to get my homey back. I'd rather had been broke than to lose my friend, my brother, my nigga.

Sitting in the opposite pew across from us was Leon's father in his tight gray suit and arched eyebrows, planted in the arms of his gay lover. They were both crying loud and dramatically. I wanted to punch that nigga in the face because he was never there for my nigga. All them tears didn't mean shit to me. That motherfucker is part of the reason my nigga was all fucked up in the head.

I took light steps up to the golden casket. I inhaled, placed my hand on the casket and whispered, "Your secret is safe with me my nigga. I'll take it to my grave." I closed my eyes and channeled memories of me and my nigga in better days and I smiled at the good times. I held a low conversation with him and ended it with telling him that this wasn't good bye and that I'd see him again.

I wiped my tears and as I was returning to my seat, I saw Nicky entering with dark black glasses against her tears, bringing in white flowers to Leon's family. She hugged them and paid her respects. As soon as she saw me, she hit the exit quick, and left. Something inside me wanted to run after her, but I had to be there for my homies. Terror and J-boy were sitting behind me and they were both crying silently. The two of them weren't taking things too well. When I explained what happened to Leon, J-Boy had especially been very stand-offish ever since.

After the wake, we held the burial at the Cedar Grove Cemetery on American Legion Highway and after, the family went to Leon's grandmother's house to eat. His grandmother was known for making the best soul food around. Cooking the massive meal helped her keep her mind off of her loss. J-Boy sat on the couch next to one of Leon's uncles and he had a stale look on his face. He pushed his black hat over his dreads down to his eyes and I went over to approach him. Squatting on the edge of the couch next to him, I needed to vent. We had lost one of our soldiers and we needed to be tighter than ever before. My stomach was still in knots and all this fuckin' stress was making my head hurt.

"J-Boy dog, this shit is hard for me man. I literally saw him take himself out. I keep seeing that shit replaying in my head over and over every time I close my eyes just like I did with my pops. All of this shit we did out here wasn't worth losing Leon dog."

"You got that shit right!" He lifted his head and burrowed his eyes in my direction. The look in his eyes were cold. He didn't say a single word to me, he bolted up and left the house.

Terror watched the whole ordeal play out. He squat next to me on the couch.

"I gotta' talk to you for a second, let's go over here." He led me to a quiet corner.

I spoke first. "Yo', did you see that shit? What was that about? What's up with this nigga J-Boy?" I was confused. I wasn't the enemy, and I didn't understand what this nigga's problem was.

Terror shook his head. "Yo', I'm your right hand man so I'm gonna' keep it a hunnet with you. That nigga J-Boy thinks that you could've done something to help Leon. He thinks you waited too long at the stop light and that you should've ran out, jumped in Leon's car, scooped him and kept it moving. You know I'm more realistic than that nigga, I know that you couldn't have gotten to that nigga in time. Shit, we probably would've lost two homies if you would've made it to him sooner, you *and* him."

A disgruntled look took over my face. How the fuck was this motherfucker J-boy blaming me for losing my nigga?

"So you're saying that nigga thinks that Leon's death was my fault?"

"Shh! Leon's grandma is right there, son." Terror nodded toward where she was. She had re-entered the living room serving plates to guests.

I lowered my voice and spoke firm and clear so that my words registered with Terror. "After all the shit we been through together dog, he would actually blame me for what happened to Leon? You know that shit was out of my control. I'm a loyal nigga, if I could've saved him, I would've. That's fucked up that a nigga in my own crew would think some dumb shit like that. J-boy's done dog, he's cut off!"

"Man stop that shit, we are all we got now. We gotta' be tighter than we've ever been. You're like my brother! You and J-boy are both my brothers, I ain't got no family nigga. You know that! We just lost one of our brothers and both of y'all are trying to destroy the family even more. Nah' dog, it can't happen." He nodded.

"It just did." I walked off and made my way to the porch. I had made up my mind that I was done with J-Boy. As I stepped on the porch, I noticed J-Boy's mom smoking a cigarette by herself on a solid white bench next to the steps on the porch. She wiped her moist eyes with a tissue and forced her large black flimsy hat out of her face. She watched all of us grow up so it seemed that she took Leon's death just as hard as everyone else.

"You okay Ant?" She asked me.

"Nah, I'm not."

"Come sit down over here next to me." She pat the bench and I hesitated before I sat.

She took a deep breath and I could feel her staring at me as I sat with my head hung low.

"You know child, I could never find the right time to talk to you about your mom and dad. This has always been something hard for me to talk about."

I shot her a look. Now she had my full attention. She took a few drags from her cigarette, I guess she was collecting the courage to speak. Once she opened her mouth, she purged out information that I should've been told years ago.

"I know you've heard rumors about your dad on the streets. Well most of them are true. Your dad was very much into crime back in the day and your mom tried her best to stick by him. He was so in love with her Ant, he tried to give her the life that she never had since they both grew up poor. Raising you was hard and they tried to do what they could but they were really struggling Anthony. Your father was determined to take care of his family, that man had the determination of a lion. One day, he and the notorious White brothers, robbed a bank in Brockton. They got away with stealing almost a half a million dollars. Rumor had it, the White brothers tried to leave Boston without giving your father his cut. When they turned up dead, everyone knew that your father had to have done it, however the money was never recovered. Your mom felt guilty because of the rumors about your dad killing the White brothers. She didn't know what to do with herself, especially when rumors surfaced that she had been cheating on your dad with one of them. Your father was absolutely devastated, but he didn't want to abandon his family. Especially because..."

Tears collected at her eyes. "What Aunty, because what?"

With tears streaming down her face, she took my hands and squeezed them tight. "I'm your mother Ant."

I snatched my hands away and stepped up and away from the bench. "Fuck you talkin' bout?" I was confused.

"Your father cheated on your mom with me. She was raped at a young age and was told that she would never be able to bear children. She was so in love with your father, our affair devastated her. I was young and dumb and begged her to forgive me because she was my best friend and I promised her that I'd end the affair immediately. Soon as I did, I found out that I was pregnant with you. I wasn't in any position to raise a child at the time so your mom and dad agreed to raise you. She adored you Ant and so did I, that's why I always used to come by and visit when she left y'all and pretend to be an Aunty figure. I felt obligated to be there for you. Two years later, she got pregnant with your sister Lea. The doctor said that Lea was considered a miracle baby since your mom wasn't supposed to be able to conceive because of the rape."

My mind was overflowing with confusion but I continued to hear her out.

"After your father robbed that bank, your house was being raided all the time and your mom was constantly being stalked by the White brother's family and she couldn't take it anymore, she feared for her life. One night, she called me in tears and said she had to get away and that she would eventually come back for you and Lea. When she met that white guy, he showed her the life that she had always dreamt about living and she wanted to bring you and Lea into her world. But when she tried to come back for you and your sister, your father wasn't having it, he was too angry at her for abandoning her family. He also didn't accept any of the money that she tried to send to you guys over the years."

"Nah' man, I don't believe that, I don't believe none of this shit."

"Believe it Ant, J-boy is your brother."

As her last words left her lips, J-boy was walking up the stairs to the porch. "I'm his what?" He asked pausing in mid-step.

She pat the bench. "We need to talk son."

J-Boy sat down next to her and I had to go. I didn't want to hear anymore. I darted down the stairs and rushed into my car. I didn't want to believe what she had told me, it couldn't be true. How could Lea be my step-sister and how could the woman that I hated for leaving me all these years not even be my real mom? Shit was surreal!

I understood that my father harbored resentment toward my mom for leaving and it was admirable of him to raise us by himself, but he could've at least allowed her to be a part of our lives. At least for Lea's sake. To me, they *both* did things wrong but it was still no excuse for my so-called mom not to fight for us.

Full of emotion, I entered the crib and stared at our family picture. I snatched it off the marble coffee table and spit venom. "Why the fuck didn't you tell me she wasn't my mother man? What the fuck kinda' shit is that pops?! Huh? You wasn't supposed to keep no shit like

124

this from me man!" I tossed the picture on the couch and squat down beside it. I felt betrayed, it was clear that my entire life was a lie. I felt so lonely and so empty. Here I was with more money than I could count but none of it mattered because I wasn't happy. I literally had no one to help me deal with these perils of life at this moment.

I continued to sit there and think. It was hard for me to gather myself but I knew that I had to, especially when I heard movements in Lea's bedroom. I approached her room and spotted her sitting on the edge of her bed dressed in all black. Apparently Donte's funeral was also held the same day as Leons. She stared at the floor while tears fell effortlessly down her cheeks. Her ponytail was disheveled and she constantly placed the tissue to her face to wipe her eyes and nose. Squatting down on the bed beside her, for the first time, I didn't know what to say to console her. Her heart was broken to pieces and my sister was like my twin, so when she hurt, I hurt. She'd been crying ever since the ordeal with Donte happened and hadn't spoken to me since.

"I can't believe this happened," she cried almost hyperventilating. She held her chest as it was caving in and out. I placed my hand on her shoulder to console her and she cried hard into her tissue.

"I'm so sorry sis. Shits been ugly out here. I mean, you know I didn't like that nigga and I didn't want you being with him but…"

She cut me off and faced me. "BUT you can't help who you fall in love with. Like I told you before. I tried to cut him off for you bro, but my heart was attached to him. Why out of all people did Leon have to kill Donte? Why Anthony, huh? I'm so heartbroken right now, I don't know what to do with myself! I loved him so much." She covered her face and cried excessively into her hands. I wanted to comfort and console my baby sister, but I knew secretly she blamed me for his death.

125

"Sis look at me. This wasn't supposed to happen, you know me better than this. I've done reckless shit out in these streets, shit I'm not proud of, but I never told Leon to kill Donte, you hear me?" Finally, I reached over to embrace her because her tears didn't stop cascading down her swollen brown face. I hated seeing her in such a fragile state. My baby sister was beyond hurt and it was fuckin' me up. Astonishingly she embraced me back. I held her tight and hoped that she could overcome the resentment she was harboring toward me for what happened and realize that I only had her best interest at heart.

I rocked my sister in my arms, she was completely torn apart.

"Before pops died, he asked me to take care of you, remember that? I wouldn't do anything to break your heart sis. I risk myself every day out in these streets for you to be straight, and for your future to be stable. But I'm beginning to re-evaluate shit. I had a goal to reach and although I'm almost there, I think it's time for me to start doing things right and leave the game now. I think it's over for me Lea, I'm gonna' pick up my last drop, push this shit out and I'm done. I got more than enough money tucked away for us. I'm hanging up the game, moving us away and opening up a business. Maybe I'll buy a car dealership and sell the type of cars that pops used to dream of driving. Remember all the expensive cars he used to talk about?"

Lea giggled through her tears and sniffed. "I remember." She sat up and looked at me. "I had my own dreams Ant. You know how much I love doing hair. Donte was gonna' quit that pimp shit and we were gonna' open up a barber shop and beauty salon together." When she mentioned his name, she began to cry until she ran out of steam. "Remember when I kept telling you that I had something to tell you but I never got around to say it?"

"Yeah." I said.

"Well I'm pregnant with Donte's baby. We planned to open up a legit business together and start our family. I've always dreamt of having the family we never had Ant. I wanted my child to have a mom *and* dad around. Now my child is gonna' be a statistic, it won't have a father!"

I was completely taken aback. When Lea rubbed the small pudge in her belly, I realized that it was real. "You're pregnant?" I asked still in disbelief.

"Yes." She whimpered. "Your boy Leon made me a single mom. Now Donte won't be able to watch his child grow up. I'm not going to none of the doctor's appointments by myself, I just can't do it. I feel so alone! So Alone!" She cried.

"You don't have to go by yourself and you're not alone, you got me. You know I'm here for you, always have been, always will be little sis! We are a unit, like pops always said, 'Anthony and Lea'."

She shot up off the bed. "No! Fuck, *'Anthony and Lea'*! Why couldn't *Anthony* just let me be happy? My life is fuckin' ruined now! How could you go with me to doctor appointments knowing that you were partly responsible for killing my child's father? I don't know if I could ever forgive you for this!" She screamed out! She gave me one final look of disgust and then ran out of the room, slammed the door and took my heart with her.

Chapter 12

I hadn't seen my sister in two long weeks. She wasn't answering my calls and I honestly had no idea where she was. The crew was laying low after Donte's death just in case his niggas tried to retaliate. We were hardly speaking, especially me and J-Boy, but we were still getting money together and best believe we had something for them niggas if they wanted to bring the smoke.

The investigation in the hood was hot because detectives found one of the spreadsheets in Leon's car the day he died. The streets began talking, and although they couldn't pinpoint who we were, they referred to us as, the *notorious pill smugglers*. The hood was riddled with cops more than ever. Niggas in the hood were getting killed off regular street beef but the police were trying to place all the blame on the *notorious pill smugglers*. All the heat from the jakes in the hood has us moving shit slower. I still hadn't gotten off my last supply so that I could pick up my last drop from the connect and give the game up.

I met up with Terror in Avon to discuss my exit plan. I told him that once I hit the connect for the last supply, I was gonna' get it off and I was out. He seemed to be convinced that the money was too good to walk away from, so I explained that I'd either put him on with the connect so he could take over the operation or he could be smart and be done with this shit too. I'd never leave my niggas out here clear and dry but I encouraged him to get the fuck out now that shit was hot. It was time for a normal life without having to watch our backs. But the money had him addicted.

"Dog, we making too much money to just walk away Ant. The numbers that you are getting for the pills now are too good to be true.

Walking away from it now isn't wise, matter fact my G, it's *stupid*, real talk."

"Well let it be stupid my nigga. I ain't letting my pops die in vain. We made enough money. Being greedy will be the death of us. You and J-Boy don't wanna' listen to shit! I'm out here helping everyone else out and I put everyone on, but who's looking out for me? Huh Terror, answer that shit?"

Terror looked away.

"I thought so. No one!" I answered my own question.

"Is it Nicky? That bitch got you falling in love, now you trying to leave niggas?"

"Watch your mouth, she ain't no bitch!" I found myself defending Nicky automatically which was something I'd never done for a woman other than Lea. No matter how mad at her I was, she wasn't the type to deserve to be disrespected, I still had a soft spot for her that I couldn't fight and I really missed her. "And you know me better than that. I would never get out the game over no pussy. It's just time nigga. You gotta' know when to recognize the expiration date when you hustle."

"Man you a sell-out if you give up the game Ant, never thought I'd see the day that you would let shit affect your hustle."

"Call it what you want dog. I ain't your bitch so I don't have to sit out here explaining myself to you. The streets are hot, Leon is gone, what the fuck else gotta' happen for y'all niggas to leave the hood?"

"There's too much money out here to get man, so I ain't going nowhere. Do you dog." He said with his head up. Disdain was all in his expression. There was only so much I could do for niggas. If he didn't want to get out, then I'd connect him with the plug and look out for me

129

and Lea. It was time for me to be selfish, I wasn't happy and I looked forward to a new beginning. The streets were too hot and being greedy was usually every hustling nigga's downfall and I refused to let it be mine. It was the end of the road for me. I didn't give a fuck who liked it. I just wanted my sister back on my team, I hadn't even gotten a chance to tell her what J-Boy's mom told me about pops.

All the stress had me missing Nicky like shit. I had been thinking about her every single day but I was too stubborn to reach out. Over the weekend I saw pictures that she posted on Instagram of the party her mom threw for her to celebrate her new publishing deal. That Instagram page that Leon had created finally came in handy because Nicky's page was private. Her poetry book was titled, *Love Him Beyond What He Can Offer You* and subtitled, *How to Love A Man The Right Way*. My stomach dropped and I felt like a piece of shit. Clearly her title alone explained why she was using the books I was tripping on for research. The last picture she posted on Instagram was a beautiful selfie with the natural lighting beaming into her brown mesmerizing eyes and her caption read, "I miss him." I knew her words were meant for me and I made it my duty to let her know in person that I had missed her too. I was only torturing myself being without her. I put my pride aside because I felt like I owed her an apology. First for tripping over the dumb shit with the books, and second, for accusing her of fuckin' with J-Boy.

Roaming through the city, I searched every flower store for white roses and when I found them, I bought her three bouquets full. I wanted her to know that shit was real this time and that I was ready to let her in. I headed up to the pharmacy to see if I could catch her but her boss said that she had missed her shift two days in a row. It wasn't like Nicky to skip out on work without at least calling first and although I didn't want to pop up at her crib unannounced, I stopped by out of concern. I had hoped that she didn't leave town to go follow her dreams that she was so passionate about. I definitely wanted to catch up to her before she made that decision. I landed three hard knocks on her door. When no one answered, I peeked over to see if her car was in the lot and it was. I heard the TV on from the front door so I assumed she was inside.

"Nick, open the door, it's Ant, I wanna' talk to you." I knocked a few more times. "Come on Nick, damn, you really got a nigga out here feeling like I'm begging, what's good?"

I assumed she was probably in the shower and didn't hear me so I called her cell, but I heard it ringing inside her house. Her walls were so thin, she would have definitely heard it ringing from the shower. Something seemed really strange. I took out my ATM card and picked through her lock and barged my way in.

"Nick!" I called out again. I followed the sound of the TV which was coming from inside her bedroom. Upon entering, I noticed Nick was curled up on her bed facing the wall. I sat beside her and shook her shoulder. "Nick wake up, it's Ant." I stood up to turn off her TV. "Nick, wake up, it's your man. I want my girl back" Slowly I rolled her over by her shoulder, I noticed her face was pale and light blue. Her body was stiff to the touch and it fucked me up. I quickly looked around and saw the residue from the mollies on her dresser and a large quantity of X pills beside it. It was painfully obvious that she had mistakenly overdosed.

"Wake up, wake up Nicky! What the fuck!" I shook her body but she was unresponsive. Her entire body was blue, she felt freezing cold to the touch and her skin felt like wax. I searched around her crib for a phone number to one of her relatives but I didn't even know what to say if I found someone to call. It was no denying it, Nicky was dead. Part of me felt like losing her was my fault. I felt like I enabled her addiction by introducing her to the shit even if it wasn't willingly. She had way more potential than losing herself to pill popping, her future was bright as daylight. I clutched her in my arms and cried like a bitch.

"Nicky baby! Damn! What the fuck did you do to yourself man!" My tears fell into her hair as I clutched her in my arms. I grew angry with her, then I got sad and then angry again. I couldn't believe I was losing someone else, shit wasn't fair.

"Wake up baby, I got white roses for you, see, I listened to you Nicky. I listened this time baby. I got it right. You can't leave me man, I don't got nobody out here man! Nobody! Why the fuck is this happening to me again! What the fuck man!" I hollared. My cries held a build-up of pain and anger. All the bad in my life was outweighing the good and I was running out of things to live for. Holding her in my arms was confirmation that I was alone.

"You're all I got out here Nick man. How could you leave a nigga? You told me that you wasn't going to leave, you said you had my back Nick! DAMN!"

I'd never taken a girl seriously before EVER, but I held her close to my heart. That very moment was the first time I felt the real emptiness of not having my mom around. I finally realized that a woman's love was something that every boy and every man needed. Women were our rib, our other half, our companion. And there I was holding mine, lifeless in my arms. Nicky had real love for a nigga like me and I too had love for her. I kissed her stiff lips, laid her down on her bed and whispered, "I love you," as tears left me.

I love you were words that I had never said to a woman besides my sister. And surprisingly, I really actually meant it. I felt it deep in my gut and even deeper in my heart. I really loved Nicky and I was going to miss her. Once again, I felt lonely, abandoned and powerless. Things went from sugar to shit real quick and I didn't have anyone to help me pick up the pieces. I didn't even have my sister to call to vent to. There was nothing that was going to help mask the pain I was feeling. I dialed 911 from Nicky's phone and left it face down on her mahogany bureau. I laid the white flowers down beside it when I noticed a white object on top of a pink box and I picked it up. It was a positive pregnancy test! I dropped down to my knees and cried so hard, I felt my stomach caving in. Not only did I lose Nick, but I also lost my unborn.

"Why didn't you tell me man! I would've been here Nick, I would've helped you! This wasn't supposed to happen baby. Why did you do this to yourself!" It took everything in me to conjure up enough energy to leave Nicky's side but I had to get ghost before the police showed up. I raced home and sat in my grief for about a week straight. I didn't change clothes, I wasn't getting money nor was I answering my phone. All I could find myself doing was shedding fuckin' tears, stressing and smoking. I've always heard about people falling into a deep depression but I really didn't know what it felt like till I went through it myself.

Word about Nicky's death traveled fast and I heard that her mom took it hard. I felt like I was also losing myself but I also knew that I'd have to pull myself together and snap out of that depressed state. I knew that wherever my sister was, she needed me at my best and that it wasn't all about me and my emotions. My phone had been ringing off the hook since I'd been off the radar. I decided to answer one of J-Boy's calls on this particular day just in case he had to tell me some shit about my sister. He and I really hadn't had a decent conversation other than about money after that shit he pulled the day of Leon's funeral.

"What up?" I answered.

"What up Ant? I heard about what happened to Nick, you a'ight?" He asked.

I sighed. "Nah'. But I'll be good." I peered at myself in the bathroom mirror, I had a light beard growing in and I looked rough and scruffy. I paused and retracted the turn of recent events and voiced them to J-Boy.

"First my pops, then Leon, now Nick. I'm done with this street shit, I don't want one of us to be next, we got too much money not to make better choices. I'm sure Terror probably told you that I'm out after this last drop."

"Yeah he told me. You serious about that?" He asked.

"Dead serious my nigga. I just want a normal life, we too old for this hood shit, it's time to give it up. You should take your doe and go open up those clothing stores we talked about. Put all that fashion shit you like to fuck with, to use. The time is now my nigga."

"I feel you. But I just can't give it up just yet tho'." He confessed.

I paused and turned my back to my bathroom mirror. "So your moms told you about that shit with her and my pops?"

He huffed. "Yeah she told me. I guess we are brothers foreal huh?"

"Yea, I guess so." I said.

"Man Ant. I'm sorry about the bullshit I pulled man, I was trippin'. We are family, same mother or not, you've always felt like blood. I know you couldn't do nothing about Leon. It just hurt losing him man, I miss him dog." I heard J-Boy stifling his cry.

"I know. I miss him too. I wish he were here to hang this shit up and leave the hood with me. I'm gonna' meet the conneezy and get up with you and Terror for your cut of this last thang." I said speaking in codes.

"A'ight my G, just hit me up and tell me when and where. I'm there."

"One."

134

I hung up and peeled off my gray jeans and blue T-shirt that I had worn for a week and I jumped in the shower. The water beamed down on my face as visions of Nicky flashed through my mind. I wondered how long she knew she was pregnant and a nigga got weak. I almost threw up as the reality of losing her hit me even harder. I let tears flow out in the shower as I fought to get my mind right.

After my shower, I felt a little refreshed, but I knew it was going to take a while for me to fully get back to being myself. I threw on my black Adidas jogging suit and grabbed my hat. I heard the front door open and I slipped on my sneakers and went to see who it was.

Walking in with round Chanel glasses to cover her puffy eyes was my sister Lea. Astonishingly, she dropped her purse and ran to hug me.

"I heard about Nicky, I'm sorry bro." She sympathized.

"Thanks. She was pregnant."

"Yeah, I heard that part too, I'm so sorry Anthony. You would've made the dopest father."

"I appreciate that Lea."

"I missed you." She broke into a loud cry and hugged me again.

"I missed you too, everything okay, how are you feeling?" I asked her.

"I'm okay, just a little sick. Where are you going?" She asked as I went to pick up my phone off the coffee table.

"I told niggas I'm making one more drop and I'm out the game. I did this for us Lea, now I'm hanging it up for us."

She took off her glasses and her eyes smiled at me.

"Before I leave, I gotta' kick it to you about something real quick."

"What's wrong?" She asked concerned.

135

I went on to explain to her about what J-Boy's mom told me about our dad, the White Brother's the robbery and the fact that the mom we've always known to be *my* mom, really wasn't. She placed her hands to her opened mouth in shock and cried excessively. I don't know if it was the pregnancy making her super sensitive but she did more crying than speaking the whole time.

"All this time we didn't have the same mom Ant?" She questioned

"Nope. Shit is wild." I answered. "I'll talk more about it when I get back."

Her beautiful, sensitive brown eyes met mine. "I don't give a fuck about having the same mother, you are my whole brother and my only family, this changes nothing. I love you Ant."

"I love you too sis." I smiled.

"*Anthony and Lea* right?" She asked with sad eyes.

"Forever." I said. "I'll be back."

Feeling like I had my sister back on my team had me feeling a little lighter. It gave me a boost of energy knowing that I had my soldier back. I opened the front door and clicked my car doors opened. As I grew closer to my car, I heard a deep voice sound out from behind me.

"Yo' Ant?" The voice seemed familiar.

When I turned around, I noticed it was the Fat Joe looking nigga from that night at the club. The same nigga that tried to run up in my old crib with his crew. He had a gun pointed toward me and his forehead was wrinkled and the expression on his face was dripping with vengeance.

"What? You came over this bitch to try to rob me nigga? You didn't learn from the first time?"

136

"I didn't come to rob you, I told you it's personal nigga!" He cocked his gun back and grinned.

"So what the fuck do you want motherfucker'?"

"I want your head! I'm Rob White, your pops killed my father *and* uncle, the White brothers. So it's a must that I take you out."

"Annnnt!!!" Lea cried from the front door. Shocked by her shouts, the gunner aimed the gun toward Lea and I reached for mine on my waist and started letting off into his torso before he could pull his trigger. Quickly, he turned and ran in the opposite direction. I chased behind him licking four shots his way. BOOM! BOOM! BOOM! BOOM!

"Come on Lea!" She hurriedly ran to my car and we crammed ourselves inside and I skid away.

"Who the fuck was that?" She asked. I could see her visibly shaking.

"That's one of the White's Brother's sons. The nigga's I was just telling you J-Boy's mom told me about. Nigga tried to come and retaliate for what pops did to his family."

"What the fuck Ant! I'm scared." She cried.

"Don't worry about it sis. I'm meeting the connect to get this last drop to bring to niggas. Fuck it, they can have the whole thing, I don't need it. It's over! We are out of here for good and we are leaving tonight." Lea sat back in her seat holding her stomach. She was facing the window crying. I leaned over to rub her shoulder to assure her that I had her back and everything was okay. When I got far enough away from the crib, I swerved the car over. I immediately wiped my prints off my gun, I didn't know if I had killed that nigga or not but I tossed it down a random sewer.

Lea had finally calmed down by the time I got to the location of my connect in Quincy. I never liked doing business with her in the car but I had to move fast.

I had already explained to my plug that after this drop, they'd be dealing directly with J-Boy and Terror from now on. With ease, they respected that I wanted out. We had a good run, no drama and no bullshit so there were no issues. We exchanged money for product and I placed it in the trunk and headed out to meet my niggas.

Upon drawing nearer to the meeting place, I grabbed my phone to text J-Boy and Terror to let them know that I'd be pulling up shortly. I kept watching my back just in case that nigga Rob White or some of his niggas was around to get some get-back, and I was anxious to get this drop done. I pulled over and waited for my niggas to get there. Lea squint her eyes staring out of her window. She pressed the button to her seat to sit all the way up.

"Bro, I see Donte's mother over there, I saw her at the funeral but I didn't get a chance to tell her about the baby."

"Nah' Lea, it's too hot, I got too much shit in the car for you to bring attention to us."

"I'm just gonna' go get her phone number, she has a right to be in her grandchild's life. I'll be right back bro."

"No! You need to do that shit another time man!"

"I'll be right back Ant, chill." Against my will, Lea exited the car and darted in Donte's mom's direction.

I was pissed but I had to keep my mind focused on this transaction. I kept watching my back as I waited for my niggas who were taking too fuckin' long.

The street wasn't that crowded and it was a low key location for us to meet but something just didn't feel right. I kept shifting in my seat whispering to myself for niggas to hurry up under my breath.

Within minutes, I saw J-Boy and Terror approaching by foot a ways up the road. We never liked to park near each other when we were making exchanges to avoid looking hot. Suddenly, nearing sounds of sirens were heard from a distance but in the hood, sirens were the norm. But this time, shit wasn't normal at all. The sounds grew nearer and I could see the flashing lights aiming my way. My stomach dropped. "Aw shit!" I shouted. Instantly, I put my key into the ignition and was about to start my car but it was too late, there was no way I would be able to get away. I had all this work in the trunk and when they discovered it, I knew that I'd be cooked.

It seemed surreal as the police cars smothered the street from every direction and boxed my Beamer in. I knew exactly who they were coming for. I could see J-boy and Terror's treads come to a halt once they saw what was happening. People began gathering around to watch what was going on. Lea had stopped talking to Donte's mom and ran over to where they had me surrounded. I was totally unmoved until they pronounced my name through the intercom and instructed me to get out of the car with my hands up. I opened the door and immediately held up my hands.

Who knew how much the cops knew. I didn't know how long I was under investigation or if they were tipped off by anyone. All I knew was that I was going down!

As the officer snatched my arms behind my back and clasped the handcuffs on my forearms, the clanking of the cuffs tightening seemed to be the only noise that I heard amongst all the other bullshit that was going on. Scores of witnesses were watching the dramatic scene play out. Some were being questioned by the local news; who of course brung their cameras to witness my downfall, but most witnesses were outright too scared to give their statements and shied away from the cameras.

I heard one of the news reporters say into the camera. "The leader of the Pill Smuggling rink has been caught, taken off the streets and will be brought to justice."

Lea was crying her heart out begging the dominating officers to let me go. "Let him go!! Let my brother go!! Pleaaase!!" She cried. I could hear her yelling, but her words were faint because everything I was hearing was fading out. Two white cops were holding her back by her arms to retain her, but she put up a fight. You could tell by her tears that it was hard for her to see her brother being whisked away by the jakes.

I managed to locate my right hand man, Terror in the crowd. He seemed to be hoping not to be scoped by the detectives. I saw him tighten the strings on his black Adidas hoodie as he watched from the sideline. Then I spotted my cousin J-Boy slowly descending from the crowd to defray from being questioned or taken into custody.

I couldn't believe everything was coming to an end. Part of me wished that my team was able to save me. I felt like they were turning their backs on me but what was I expecting them to do? They couldn't rescue me from the surrounding ten to fifteen police cars that had my Beamer squared in. This wasn't a fuckin' movie and them niggas wasn't Ranbow. Yet I still couldn't grasp how I got caught, my game was virgin pussy tight, there was no way for the jakes to be on to me.

The officer placed his hand on the back of my waves and before he pushed my head down to place me in the back of the police car, I took one last look at my team; my sister, my right hand man and my cousin who I could still see walking off. My operation was fool proof, I may have been the ring leader but why was I the only one being arrested? There was no other way to answer it; one of them, was a **SNITCH!**

Chapter 13

As I sat in the backseat of the police car, I reflected on the past year. Success was an understatement. All that money had me feeling like King Tut or motherfuckin' Hercules. The world and everything in it was ours for the taking. I had the money to go anywhere I wanted to go and the cash to purchase just about anything I wanted to buy. Instead, I stayed humble in order to make a better life for my sister and an overall stable future for myself as well. I had a full team of thorough niggas, their wants and needs were met and everyone was more than comfortable when it came to this paper. The capacity of my uprising business had the potential to keep us rich forever. But on the brink of success, there was always some bullshit.

They say that money is the root of all evil and I now believe it to be true. I lost my nigga Leon, my girl, my sister's trust and my niggas were turning their backs against me and not wanting to give up the game over this money. All I wanted to do was get out the game and do shit right. No more transporting, no more moving shit and just turning everything legit. I couldn't bear to take another L. And here I was, taking the ultimate L by getting locked up.

They say those that live morally work for those that don't. The un-moral are the ones that get ahead in life. It's unfortunate but true. I've exercised bad judgment by supplying the streets with these pills but I wouldn't have ever made as much money as I did by working an honest job. I know that what I was doing wasn't right but a nigga's heart was in a good place. I just wanted all my niggas to eat and to be able to honor my pop's word and take care of my sister. I didn't deserve to go out like this.

I sat back and placed my head against the wall in the cold jail cell. All sorts of thoughts were racing through my mind. I knew that I wouldn't be able to sleep until my official court date and that's exactly what happened. What I had on my side was the fact that they didn't have evidence to convict me for all the random murders in the hood. There was no way to tie me into those cases. The only thing that I could get charged for was for the briefcase of pills that they found in my trunk because that's all that I had on me. All of my money was in a safe place that they'd never find and when they raided my crib, they didn't find anything. Still, since the news had glorified the whole, *Pill Smuggling Rink* title and made it seem like I was so notorious in the hood, I knew that I'd probably get the book thrown at me for that. I acquired a good lawyer and was ready to hear my sentence so that I could get it over with. When my lawyer told me that they had someone testifying against me, that's when I got scared.

Walking into the courtroom in an oversized orange jumpsuit with my hands cuffed and my feet shackled, it was like I could smell my fate. I had the feeling that the judge was going to try to throw me *under* the jail. He was bald, black and his cold face full of wrinkles made him appear intimidating. I said a quick prayer and tried to remain optimistic. I sat down next to my lawyer with confidence.

When the judge asked the prosecutor to call their key witness to the stand, automatically my heart sunk. I don't think I've ever felt so betrayed and let down in my life, but my stomach dropped to my dick as the witness entered the courtroom. My eyes froze in disbelief because the witness was none other than my sister Lea. My heart was instantly ripped right out of my chest! She wore a plaid school girl dress as she approached the witness stand. A nigga was weak as fuck! She was crying immensely and the judge bent over to hand her a Kleenex.

Damn not Lea, I whispered to myself. I looked up at the ceiling. *Pops help me*, I whispered again. Tears welled up in my eyes, but I held them at bay. All I could do was stare; I couldn't blink, talk or move. I was in total disbelief of her disloyalty. Even my lawyer's face showed signs of sympathy for me. My nostrils were flaring, my heart was fluttering and

142

my reality was rocked, hard. I'd be damned that my sister wouldn't sit up there and start telling. Not Lea! Why would my own sister be the one to tear me down? That's when I realized that shit was a set up. I hadn't heard from my sister since the day she disappeared after she blamed me for being partly responsible for Donte's death. That's probably when she linked up with the jakes to create a plan to take me down. Coming to the crib to give me sympathy for Nicky's death and acting like nothing ever happened was all a ploy. Was she really talking to Donte's mom on the street that day or was it an informant?

Lea sat up on the stand and looked me square in the eyes. She cleared her throat and cried into the mic, "This is for Donte and for my baby." She said. The evil in her eyes beamed fire as if a different sister emerged. Her words shattered my world completely.

"Excuse me?" The prosecutor asked.

"Nothing." She said as she sunk her head down and cried. The Attorney began his questioning but Lea was crying too hard to answer any of the questions.

"Do you need a moment?" He asked her.

"No, I'm ready." She sniffed and then locked eyes with me before saying," I'm ready to talk."

"Can't believe this shit!" I whispered squirming in my seat. I peeked over my shoulder and was surprised to see J-Boy and Terror sitting in the back of the court room. Their faces mimicked the same shock as mine. I shut my eyes, put my head down and nodded. This had to be a bad dream. What kind of loyalty was this? It didn't make any sense. Not my sister, my own flesh and blood, the one that I did all this shit for in the first place! How could she be the one to betray me? To make matters worse, her reason was because of Donte, over a NIGGA! She made me wish that I *was* the one that murdered him with my bare hands if I'd known she would pull this shit on me. I wasn't even the one that killed the nigga. How could she put another nigga before me when I would do anything for her? I would die for Lea. If she needed my heart I

would cut it out myself and hand it to her. I gave my all to the streets just for her and who would have thought that she'd be the one to bury me alive. Shit just wasn't right!

With a heavy heart, I sat and watched as my sister revealed the inner workings of my operation to the court. It was like a stranger was up there. Terror and J-Boy was shook, they seemed like they wanted to leave the court room in case their names were mentioned. I saw them fidgeting in their seats but the only name that was mentioned was mine. I had no choice but to mute out everything that was being said because I was suffocating in my seat. She literally sat up there and ratted me out, plain and simple, there was no changing the words that she was revealing. She told them what I was moving, how much I was moving and how much money I was making while supplying the streets. At that very moment it was official, I would never be able to fuck with my sister EVER again and I'd never thought I would see the day that I would have to say that.

My Attorney served Lea with his line of questioning and then the judge spoke.

"Anthony Currington! Punks like you disgust me! Selling paraphernalia to the people of your own community, do you really think that you deserve freedom?" His eyes seared at me unremorsefully. "Sentencing will commence on May 16th, you better pray for leniency." BANG! The judge banged the gavel and dismissed the court. I couldn't contain my anger anymore, I was HOT! I didn't give a fuck how my performance looked to the court because I was already cooked, my sister just buried me and I couldn't let her leave the courtroom without it weighing on her conscious.

"What about pops Lea? What you think pops would say about what you just did to me? You told on your own brother, your own flesh and blood over a nigga? What happened to our bond, us against the world, right? Pops asked me to take care of you and I broke my ass for you and this is what you do? This is how you show your appreciation?

144

Fuck you! You're just like the lady that claimed to be our mother, you betrayed me over a man! You're a *snitch* Lea, a fuckin' SNITCH! Ain't no *Anthony and Lea*, you're dead to me!" Finally my tears fell loosely from my eyes as anger laced my face. My sister literally put nails in my coffin and threw me to the wolves so she needed to know how I felt. She was on her own now, there was no coming back from this.

She blocked her ears and sped out of the court room.

"Take him away!" The judge continuously banged his gavel. "Order in this court right now, take him out!"

My outbursts forced the officers to bum-rush me out of the courtroom. When they got me into the holding cell in the back, they slammed me to the ground while in cuffs and they fucked me up real good. I didn't even feel any of the blows the officers landed on my body because all I could think about was what my sister had just done to me. No beat down could ever compare to it. I was drenched in blood before I was transported back to the prison.

Luckily I had no cellmate because I needed to desperately let my anger out. I did push-ups, I punched the air, I cried silently and I Prayed. Feelings of betrayal was an understatement. Every time I thought about Lea, I had to say a Prayer to keep myself from going crazy. I paced the room for about an hour straight. Disbelief front-lined my thoughts. I kept trying to convince myself that what happened in court didn't really happen.

Memories of me and my sister as kids were replaying in my mind, how tight we were and how disappointed my pops would be if he was alive to see what she had done. He taught us better than this. I did my part by fulfilling his dying wish which was to take care of her but it got me burnt in the end. I wouldn't see the light of day for years to come after what the jakes found in my trunk on top of all the shit Lea told them. She literally sat on the stand and made it seem like it was a one man show, like I was moving all the pills by myself. I was fine with taking the wrap for my homies, my loyalty to them wasn't going anywhere; there was no need for all of us to go down. Our unit was supposed to be air tight, no cracks, no leaks. I would never had thought that anyone in my crew would rat on me, especially my own family. Snitches get stitches, isn't that the saying? But what if it's your own flesh and blood that you looked out for all your life, does that saying still apply?

I was numb in court the day of sentencing. I put my head down and prepared to hear my fate. The judge sentenced me to eight years in prison because despite all of Lea's accusations, the prosecutors couldn't prove anything. They were only able to charge me for the supply they found in my vehicle. I swallowed my mistakes and tried to digest the verdict. It was time to man up and I prepared myself to do the time.

Chapter 14

They had a nigga locked down for 22 hours a day. The two hours they let us out for rec time was still suffocating. The only thing that kept me going was the fact that I was smart enough to choose to put my money in a safe place that I'd hoped would still be there when I got out. I applauded myself for not telling Lea where the money was but all along I was saving it mainly for her in case something like this happened to me. After what she did, I'd never allow her access to it. And little did her snitch ass know, it was closer to her than she thought. I'd settled with the fact that if my money wasn't there when I got out, I'd just have to prepare myself to accept the additional L. I mean, eight years is a long time to be away from my money.

I stayed to myself because I wasn't trying to get too close to anyone. I just wanted to do my time and get the fuck out of there. Every day I would notice this old dark skinned black man with gray hair in his mustache always staring at me. I told myself that if that nigga did that staring shit another day, I was checking his ass on site, and of course he did.

I walked up on him and before I could say anything, he questioned me.

"You Thomas Currington's son?"

"Who the fuck wanna' know?" I barked.

He chuckled. "I ain't your enemy young brother, I just want to talk to you. Are you his son?"

"Yeah." I said, my eyebrows were still bent and my game face was strong. You couldn't trust anyone in prison.

"May we?" He pointed to a corner behind some niggas that were playing cards and I reluctantly followed behind him. He pushed his square glasses toward his face and leaned against the wall.

"I knew your father very well. Me and Thomas were good friends before I landed in this piss hole for life for murder." His head bent to the floor as he smiled and nodded. Seemed like he was reflecting on the past. "I heard what happened to him and it devastated me man. My deepest condolences."

"I appreciate that man." I told him.

"Thomas and I were old players, we did a *lot* of dirt together but your father was a legend."

My ears were now wide open. This was the first time besides talking to J-Boy's mom that I had heard someone telling me more about my pop's past than I had heard about on the streets.

"Your father robbed a bank when he was about your age. The White Brothers tried to fuck him out of his cut so when their bodies were found, your father was smart enough to keep his nose clean so that there was no connection. Everyone thinks the money was never recovered but your father could never talk about where it really went."

He looked around before he continued. "Your father had that money, but instead of using the money to live lavish, your father poured the money into the projects. People that were getting evicted or losing custody of their children because of their lack of income was able to keep their families together because of your father. He's a hero and always will be. He couldn't spend a dime of that money because he and your mom was always being harassed by the cops about his connection to the robbery. I think he turned to alcohol since he wasn't able to use that money to keep his own family together. He literally gave it all away so that he wouldn't go to jail. All that risk and little reward. Your father was selfless, he could have easily kept it and fled, but he used it for a good cause to help others that were struggling like himself. His heart was always so big."

"Yeah I know." I said.

He looked me in my eyes. "I heard that you were the same way, that you would give your life for yours."

"Always." I said.

He smiled. "We got your back in here, you don't have to worry about nothing. You're Thomas Currington's son, a legend." He dapped me up and I felt the love through our exchange.

When I got back to my cell, I realized how much I was like my pops. It was almost natural for me to look out for people I loved. That's why I went so hard for my sister and for my niggas, even when niggas wouldn't do the same for you. I was loyal and it went without saying.

****

Prison time was moving in slow motion. Not a single solitary motherfucka' hit me up or consistently visited me for the first four years that I was locked up. Neither of the women who claimed to be my "mom" ever visited, wrote a letter or cared to share a single FUCK in the world for me. J-Boy never visited once and Terror who was supposed to be my right hand man, didn't visit me either. I was literally on my own. It hurt not receiving letters or support from them niggas after all that bread I broke with them.

I always prayed for my niggas though. I still have and always will have love for them. I knew they didn't think like me so over the years I prayed that they would be safe and wise enough to take their money and move their families out the hood for good. Just like I encouraged them to do. Being greedy would only land them where I was and unfortunately, I found out just recently, it did.

For some reason it seemed like anything that happened on the streets, hit the jails at lightning speed. We always knew who got killed, whose house got raided or who got locked up, immediately. My cellmate crossed his diesel arms and raised one foot up against the cement wall and told me that the jakes got my niggas. All I could do was

149

nod and put my head down. I felt their pain but I was angry at them for not listening to me. They had a chance to move away with their freedom and a shit load of money, but it turns out, they would be facing a more significant sentence than I was given. My sentence was small time compared to what they were about to face. My cellmate explained that both J-Boy and Terror got caught with not only pills, but large quantities of heroin, weed and cocaine too. I heard Terror also had a bunch of guns in his possession. Here I was with four years left and my niggas hadn't even been sentenced yet. I was pissed because they didn't even have to push all that shit in the hood, they had enough money to leave. They hated when I preached about that greedy shit but it ultimately turned out to be their downfall. And although I was angry, I was devastated for my niggas and if they were transferred to my prison once they got sentenced, I'd have their backs like nothing changed.

   "*ANTHONY CURRINGTON*, you have a letter!" The C.O. hollared out slipping the letter into my cell. I picked it up and my cellmate exited the cell for rec time. I had no idea who the letter was from since no one had written me since I had been inside. I turned it over and saw my sister's name written in blue ink and instantly my defenses went up. I almost didn't wanna' fuckin' open it. I was still disgusted by her disloyalty. The hate I harbored for her was unreal and I never thought I'd see the day that I felt so much hatred for my baby sister. I squat down on the hard ass mattress on my bunk and hesitated before I opened it. I huffed and then ripped through the seal and was surprised that it only included two short paragraphs.

The letter read...

   My dear brother, I'm probably the last person you wanted to hear from but I had to write you to tell you how sorry I am for what I've done to you. You are the last person in this world that deserves to be where you are and I have to live with what I did to you every day. I keep the picture of us with pops on top of pop's old TV in my new apartment because y'all are the only men that really loved me and probably ever will. You were right about Donte, I found out that he had two other bitches pregnant the same time that I was pregnant and I really should've listened to you bro. He was actually engaged to one of the girls. I feel really stupid! I just wanted to let you know that if you had revenge on your heart for me, you can put it to sleep. That bitch named karma already paid me a visit in the worst way. You see bro, I had never went to a single doctor's appointment because I didn't want to go through my pregnancy experiences without Donte by my side. But when I delivered my son, it was revealed through blood tests that I had the monster. Yes, I'm HIV positive.

Remember when you severely broke my nails from seeing Donte the day that daddy died? Well I guess all of the blood from daddy's wound when he shot himself sank into my open wounds when I was holding him and I never knew that I had it. I guess you paid me back and you didn't even know it. Not sure if the other women he got pregnant or their kids have it too, but my son, your nephew, was infected through childbirth. I have included a picture of him in the envelope and he looks just like you bro. I just wanted to say that if you have any love left for me, Pray for me, Pray for us...
It's still Ant and Lea for Life!

I dropped the letter and shot off the bed away from it like it was poison. My eyes protruded from my face because the letter left me confused. Thoughts were stirring inside my head rapidly transferring into an instant headache. I was in total shock! My sister was now living with a death sentence and there was nothing she could do about it. I dropped down to my knees and prayed for her *and* for my nephew. I even prayed that this grudge and all this anger and resentment I was feeling in my heart for her would eventually subside.

I bent to take the picture of my nephew out of the envelope and the brown skin, round head little boy was a handsome little nigga. If shit was differently, I would have been out there spoiling that little nigga rotten and making sure my sister didn't have to worry about shit. I stuck the picture next to my bunk with a piece of gum and stared at it.

Unfortunately I don't think that all the praying or meditation would help me heal from the scars of my sister's disloyalty but he was innocent. My sister on the other hand, bit the very hand that fed her. She selfishly sucked the soul out of the only person that would have never betrayed her. If it wasn't for her, I wouldn't even be sitting in the belly of the beast with a bunch of crab ass niggas I didn't know, I'd be free.

Laying flat on my bunk, I melted my eyes into the ceiling. Visions of Nicky and her beautiful smile surfaced. I could still hear her melodic laugh and her voice calling my name in her angelic accent. *"Hey Anthony, I missed you Papi."* I smiled at the thought of her. She was literally that one person that was in my corner foreal. She had real love for a nigga, she would have never done to me what my sister done to me and I missed her with every fiber of my being.

I felt foolish. I was so busy worrying about providing for Lea and making sure my homies were straight, I wasn't really focused on the one person that I should've been focused on, Nicky. She kept trying to get me to see that what we had was real, but yet and still, I neglected her because of my selfish issues with love and trust. Lea was grown, she sought after the love she craved for from Donte but I never gave Nicky my all like I should have. I sought love from my sister and from the streets when all along it was given to me effortlessly from Nicky at no charge. It was that rare, innocent, real love in the purest form, just as she used to describe the white roses that she loved so much. I should've recognized that the emotional connection we had was real, genuine and authentic. It's a shame that it took for my sister and my homies to turn their backs on me to realize that my energy was in the wrong place. All the feelings that I couldn't recognize when I was with Nicky was love, it was love that I was neglecting and it was love that I should've embraced.

I turned and glanced over at the picture of my little nephew and I imagined what it would have been like if Nicky were alive and we had our child together. Suddenly sadness overcame me. The pit of my stomach sank low and I felt bouts of grief inside me, trying to force out my emotions. I discovered a single tear leaking from my right eye. I sat up and removed my nephew's picture from the wall. He was at Franklin Park posed with his arms crossed in front of a tree that had a black parked bench behind it. As I examined the picture closer, I noticed an older white woman sitting on the bench. It was hard to see her face because she was looking in the opposite direction. But I couldn't help but notice what was in her lap. It was a bouquet of white roses facing in the direction of the picture. That shit blew my mind! I felt like it had to be a sign from Nicky. I think she was trying to tell me that everything was gonna' be alright and that she was still with me. I viewed the picture more closely because that shit freaked me out, but in a good way and I wiped my tear and smiled. I realized that my Angel was still watching out for me and it gave me a sense of comfort.

Suddenly her words came to mind. *"I'm never giving up on you until the day you love me back. And when you do, that's when everything will make sense."*

I never knew how much bearing her words would have on my future, but she was right. I now realize how deep the love is that I had for her, and now, everything does make sense. I had already fulfilled my pop's dying wish a long time ago. I had already made enough money for my sister's future, it was up to Lea to go in whatever direction she chose to go in. Naively, I didn't realize that I had to let her fly and live her own life. I couldn't control who she loved but I should have controlled who I chose to love. All this time, it should've been *Anthony and Nicky*, not *Anthony and Lea*, but now it's too late.

I know Nicky's in heaven with my unborn child with no worries and I will never forget what she taught me.

I laid back and reflected on my life as a whole and realized that there had to be some permanent changes from here on out. It was time for me to grow up. All I ever did was try to live by the code of the streets. What the rapper Rick Ross say? *"A boss is one who guarantee we gon' eat."* I held my niggas down, we ate together, I never snitched and I always stayed loyal. They say when shit hit the fan, either the real or the fake in niggas close to you will reveal itself and unfortunately, that's what happened. In particular, my sister really showed her hand. She showed me who she really was, fake as fuck! Still after four years of me being locked down, and knowing now that karma has already paid her back, I still can't get over what she did to me. She wasn't supposed to turn her back on me over a nigga. Although I couldn't knock her for seeking the type of love that I couldn't provide for her, she shouldn't have betrayed me in the process, that shit just wasn't real, you should never go against the family! I finally realize that all this time, I was loyal to the wrong girl and I should've been completely loyal to Nicky and accepted her love because it was the one thing in this world that I had never felt until I met her. And although it was brief, it felt right.

8 Years of my life, I can NEVER get back! But thank GOD, a nigga made it!

Chapter 15 –*The End of My Sentence…*

To heal a wound, you have to stop touching it… -Tupac

I can't believe eight years blasted by and I only had two weeks left in prison. My hair had grown out into a nappy fro and I was officially part of the beard gang. Every time I stole glimpses of myself in the plastic prison mirrors, I felt like I was looking more and more like my pops. I even saw one gray hair in the thick of my beard and it made a nigga feel old as fuck. Prison had stolen the rest of my twenties and although I felt like I grew wiser, I couldn't wait to be free so that I could live my life the way I should've lived it before I went in.

Don't get it twisted, my stent in prison wasn't smooth at all. I got into it with a few of my cellmates because new niggas always thought they were tough when they first entered prison. I had to lock-in with them to show them how these hands worked but once they found out who I was and who my father was, niggas had to respect it. Especially when they were amongst population, they were getting it way worse than the ass whoopings I gave them. I had all the respect in prison because of my pop's legacy and the fact that I didn't snitch on my team. So if niggas knew I had a problem with someone, I didn't even have to speak, I'd only have to make eye contact and the old heads would handle them for me. Other than that, I read books, worked out and prayed to pass the time by.

I became real close to a cat named Rico and a nigga named Lim. They were both black with some sort of Latin mixture. Both of these niggas were cool as fuck. Real recognize real and we just connected immediately. They were both around my age and focused on bigger shit than this hood shit when they get out.

Rico was from Mattapan, he was locked up for attempted murder. Him and his boys tried to get revenge on the niggas who killed his brother, so I felt his pain. I would've wanted revenge too! But when he caught up with the nigga who shot his brother, he popped the nigga up but he didn't die. He lived to snitch on Rico and so he was sentenced to nine years for attempted murder and possession of a firearm. He was already in prison a year before I got there and he only had a few days left.

Lim was locked up for armed robbery that he committed on a liquor store in Canton. He said he attempted the lick because he had a baby on the way and needed a quick come up. Turns out, the liquor store owner had a gun bigger than Lim had. He remotely locked Lim inside the store and held him at gun point until the police arrived. Lim's niggas was outside in the getaway car but left him once they heard the police sirens nearing. He was locked up for seven years and scheduled to get out next week.

As soon as I met them niggas, we just clicked! Not to mention we were all basically being released around the same time. I almost felt like we were meant to vibe the way we did. We were like a family in there. And I knew that once we were out, that we'd vibe the same on the outside as well. Both of their crimes involved other people and neither one of them snitched. They believed in living by the code of the streets and nigga's in jail respected their gangsta'.

Nicky's mom had been writing me for the past three months to check up on and me. I really felt like everyone had forgotten about me so it was dope to hear from someone on the outside. She knew how much Nicky meant to me and although a lot of time had gone by, we were still helping each other to heal. Nicky was my heart, I'd never felt love the way she loved me from anyone before and after eight years; I still feel her love for me the same, because it was real. I just wish that I knew how to handle it when she was still alive. It was foolish of me to run from it. Her mom would send me poems that Nicky had written to help keep my spirits up. I could tell that most of the poems were inspired by our relationship. Unfortunately, I could also see clearly how much she was crying out for help through her artistry. The pills were taking over her and I was so busy running the streets that I wasn't there for her like I should have been.

Her mom reaching out to me meant so much to a nigga like me. I had given up on people on the outside, but Nicky's mom had me feeling like there was some sense of loyalty still left in the world. She didn't have to reach out to me but she did. I could really see where Nicky got the warmth in her heart from. I made it my duty to expel how gracious I was to have her in my life. Although it had only been three months since she'd been writing, it seemed like my bid got shorter every time I received a new letter from her. I really cherished our growing friendship. I guess the feeling of never having a mother figure around had me really gravitating towards her energy. What really surprised me was when she offered to open up her home for me upon my release. The weight of the world was lifted off of my shoulders. I had been worrying myself sick about having a spot to be released to. I swear from the very first letter that I had received from her; it was like an angel had found me when I was at my lowest point. Having a place to stay was one less thing that I had to worry about.

Now that I only had two weeks left, I was just trying to pass the time by without incident. I was outside at rec kicking it with one of my old heads near the iron fence. He was a lifer and so he was preaching to me about keeping my nose clean when I get out and I soaked in the advice. While he spoke, I raised my head up at the gleaming sun and I anticipated being able to enjoy it outside of the prison quarters. I peered around at all the niggas outside, some were lifting weights, some were playing ball and surprisingly, no one was fighting. I recognized two niggas walking outside of the building together and immediately I dismissed my old head. It was my niggas, J-Boy and Terror.

157

I walked up behind them and disguised my voice. "Fuck y'all niggas with?" In unison, they turned around on the defense and once they saw my face, we all laughed.

"Fuck is good my nigga?" Terror asked dapping me up.

"My nigga Ant-Money!" J-Boy greeted me and dapped me up after.

"What's good! Damn man, I thought y'all niggas would have been here a long time ago. I heard what happened and shit." I sympathized. I had heard that they both got caught up with pills, weed, cocaine, heroin and Terror was also caught with a bunch of guns.

Both of their smiles disappeared. "Nigga, we got smoked, I got eleven years and Terror got fourteen because of the gun possession. We been locked up at Walpole and shit and just got transferred here today."

I noticed J-Boy's dreads were all different lengths and they looked damaged. He was losing his hair at the top so the front of his hair looked like short frizz and the rest of his hair looked like fried, short and long lengths of dreads. That nigga wasn't no pretty boy in them prison clothes. The dark bags under his eyes made him look stressed as fuck.

Terror shaved his head because he was losing his hair at the top. I could see shadows of where his hairline was receding. His face was covered with facial hair. I couldn't believe how many gray hairs I saw buried inside his beard. There were patches of dark acne and dry skin on his forehead, probably from the cheap soap the prison system provided. He looked scruffy and he aged badly. I assumed it was due to stress; them niggas had mad years left on their sentences.

"When do you get out?" J-Boy asked me.

"Nigga I got two weeks left."

"That's what's up man." J-Boy grinned. I couldn't tell if he was happy for me or if he wished it was him getting out.

Terror shook his head. "Don't start preaching to us about how you told us so and shit."

I nodded. "Nigga, I ain't preaching to y'all; y'all are grown ass men. We can't change the past, but going forward, I hope y'all get your minds right.

"That's true shit." J-Boy said looking down shamefully and shaking his head.

"Y'all got any money left from all that hustling y'all was doing out there?" I asked them.

"Nigga, they found our money and seized that shit!" Terror said, pounding his fist in his hand.

"Wait. So y'all niggas are telling me, y'all didn't invest, y'all didn't put no money away or nothing? I know niggas know better than that."

"Everything's gone." J-Boy admitted sadly.

All I could do was shake my head. I set the foundation for niggas to make money and better decisions, and all they did was invest it in more drugs and get caught up in the worst way. Niggas really disappointed me.

"I know we fucked up Ant. We should've listened to you and got out when you told us to, but the money and the thrill of making it was addictive. And yo', just know that I'm sorry I wasn't visiting you like I should have when we were out man, I had so much shit going on, I was just trying to stay up."

I giggled. "You were just trying to stay up huh Terror? Nigga, you're supposed to be my right hand man. And J-Boy, we are family, but niggas just straight forgot about a nigga when y'all were on the outs."

"Sorry dog. We fucked up, and now that we been locked up all this time, we know how it feels to have people just forget about you while you're in this bitch." Terror said.

"It don't feel good do it?" I felt the need to throw a jab, though I knew that when I got out, I would still make sure they were straight in the inside. I'd never leave them niggas stanking, it's just not the way that I was built.

"Yo' Ant, you good?" Lim and Rico approached us, Rico had his chest poked out.

"Oh yeah, Lim, Rico, these are my nigga's I was telling y'all about, J-Boy and Terror."

Everyone dapped each other up. I had already hipped Lim and Rico to my crew so they knew from the names who they were. J-Boy and Terror seemed to have their guard up and it was pretty apparent.

"Oh this is the fam, huh?" Lim asked sarcastically as he checked out J-Boy and Terror.

See, Lim and Rico had niggas on the outside that were putting money on their books and occasionally they'd throw me something on my books on the strength of them. I thought that was some real G shit. They didn't even know me from Adam but looked out for me. They had niggas holding them down their whole bid and they wasn't feeling the way my niggas did me. Niggas were entitled to have their opinions, but these were my niggas and this was for me to handle.

"Yea' nigga, we the fam. The *only* fam my nigga." J-Boy answered instantly jumping on the defense.

Sensing the tension getting thick, I chose to dismiss Lim and Rico so that I could finish talking about family business. "Ay' yo', let me finish kickin' it with them, I'll holla' at y'all in a minute.

"A'ight my nigga." Lim nodded as the duo walked away.

"Yo' Ant, what's good with them funny style niggas?" J-Boy asked.

"Nah they good, we been locked up in here for a good minute. They good peoples."

"Well I don't trust them. I'm sure you told them about us, they tryna' rock too hard for you like they fam' and shit. Never heard of a nigga named Lim and Rico. Where they from? Something about them nigga's seem suspect."

"Fuckin' right, them niggas ain't gang, gang, gang." Terror frowned in the direction they walked off too.

"Damn, I haven't seen y'all niggas in years and y'all already coming back around sizing niggas up and shit. Daaaamn!!!" I joked.

J-Boy and Terror finally cracked a smile. "Just stay on your toes Ant, stay woke.

"Chill my dude. Lim and Rico are good niggas, they are hot heads but they woke too." I said.

J-Boy nodded and a serious facial expression that I'd never forget covered his grill. "I'll tell you like this. I ain't getting close to nobody in this bitch. In or out of jail, I don't trust nobody! And when it comes to you Ant, I will lay **A Woke Nigga To Sleep!** Body a nigga on site for you. You are my fuckin' family. Never met a nigga realer!" J-Boy huffed.

I had to calm J-Boy down, he was just trying to prove to me that after all this time, he still had my back. But I already knew that and wouldn't expect anything less from him. "Oh you already know bro, no one's closer than fam." I quickly reminisced on how close the crew were and how we really did used to be like family and then I thought of one of our missing links. "Speaking of fam, rest in peace to that nigga Leon. Miss him every day."

"Miss my guy. Fly high." Terror said, saluting the sky.

161

The three of us continued catching up like old times as if we had never missed a beat. I really missed my niggas' and it felt refreshing to talk to them. This was the first time in eight years that the smiles and laughs I displayed in prison were genuine. It was a feeling that I had forgot I could possess. And although my niggas didn't hold me down when they were on the outs, I had missed them dudes and it was easy for me to forgive them.

A few days later was Rico's release date. He left me with all of his contact information so that we could connect once I was out. J-Boy and Terror showed no interest in seeing him off. They didn't even come out of their cells. But Lim and I were amped for him.

"Be easy out there my nigga." I said dapping him up.

"Only thing that's gonna' be easy is the pussy I'm slipping in when I hit the block, NIGGA!" He joked. The three of us shared a laugh.

"A'ight, see you on the outs man, your day is coming." Rico said as he nodded to Lim.

"One hunnet." Lim replied.

"Shit, your special day is coming too Ant." He said smiling largely at me.

"Yeah I know. See you on the outs." I told him.

Lim and I saluted him and watched as he trailed out of the prison block and head off to freedom. I was happy for my nigga, prison wasn't a place for no one. But unfortunately, my mood changed real quick at the sound of the alarm heard later that day. The entire prison got locked down because some nigga had hung himself in a cell directly upstairs from my cell. The prison kept us caged in for days like animals while they investigated that shit. We were only let out for two hours a day while we were on lock-down so unfortunately, I wasn't really able to catch up with J-Boy and Terror as much as I wanted to.

Finally they ruled dude's death as a suicide and prison was back to normal. You know, the same shit, boring and stealing minutes and hours of my life that I would never be able to get back. The upside to it was that I only had a little over a week left and I was itching to get back on the outside. Especially after Lim was released, I saluted him as they led him out and I could feel my time coming. I looked forward to kicking it with Lim and Rico on the outside, they both had the potential to do major shit. Now that they were both released, I had hoped that they would keep their noses clean until it was my time to be released.

"**Visits!!**" The C.O. announced before calling out names. I watched through the small window in my cell as niggas got called out for their visits. It used to hurt when I first got locked up because I knew that my name was never going to be called. And eventually, I became numb to it.

I heard the heavy-set C.O. call out J-Boy's name for a visit. "Must be nice." I whispered to myself.

When the visitors were escorted out to the visiting room, I called out for Terror. He was just three cells down from me, so he was able to hear me clearly.

"Yo' Terror, who's up here visiting J?"

"His ma' dukes. She been holding him down his whole bid and shit. She keep money on his canteen and the whole nine, that nigga got it smooth in here."

"Oh, word?" I replied. I squat down on my bunk and laid back. I folded my hands behind my head to think. Part of me was disappointed because she was supposed to be *my* mom too. How could she reveal that she was really my mother and *still* not hold me down? I'd been locked up for eight years and she never even showed her face, not even once. J-Boy landed there for about a week and got a visit from her ASAP. Shit like that is what made my trust for people fucked up because having someone solid in my corner was rare. That's why I respected Nicky's mom. But my so-called real *mother*, was just another

163

motherfucker I wrote off a long time ago. It was what it was, I learned that I was always going to have my own back and I was fine with it.

A few days later, I was surprised when I heard my name called for a visit. I had no idea who could be coming to visit me.

"Anthony Currington! You have a visit!" The guard pitched out as he continued to call out other names.

I stood up from the bottom bunk and my cellmate peered his eyes toward mine.

"You good Ant?" He asked.

I couldn't fight the puzzled look off my face. "Nah, I don't know who the fuck is coming up here to visit me."

My pale faced cellmate smirked and shook his head. He swiftly lifted himself up on the top bunk with his tattooed arms and sat back against the dingy wall. He had that thick white boy, South Boston accent.

"Man you just better be lucky that you are getting a visit. No one has ever came in this bitch for me and I doubt they ever will." He looked away. Instantly I felt his pain. Having no support while in prison made time go by at a snail's pace. I already felt like I was abandoned, but being abandoned in prison felt way worse.

The guard called my name again and I did as I was instructed and headed toward the visitor line. I followed through the cold hallway down to the crowded visitor's room and when I saw the face of the person visiting me, all I could do was smirk. She was just there a few days ago visiting J-Boy. Here she was, visiting me as if the shit was sincere.

My so-called *mother* walked towards me and squeezed me with a fake hug and forced a whack ass smile. She then sat across from me at the table. The awkward air circulated before us and I could tell she was nervous. The visits were conjugal so she was able to see my body language pure as day. My face hadn't changed its position; I wasn't in the mood for being fake. The woman that I thought was my mom abandoned me as a shorty and now that I knew that the woman in front of me was my real mom, she disappeared on me as a grown man.

"Wow, you look so much like your father with all that hair on your face. Still handsome as ever and you still have your boy-like features. You are just-"

I scoot myself closer to the table and looked in her eyes. "What's up?!" I cut her off. I just wasn't there for the fake shit.

She tugged on both sides of her blue sweater, sat back in her seat and cleared her throat. "Well, J-Boy told me that you were in here and I was so glad that the two of you could be in here together given the circumstances. You have always been someone he looked up to and I want you to look out for him in here. He seemed to be a little depressed at the prison he was at before he got here and I just want you to make sure he doesn't slip into that funk again. "

I chuckled. This lady had me straight twisted. I felt so disrespected! The nerve of her to let those words slip out of her full lips. "So let me get this straight. You came here to ask me to watch over J-Boy, or did you come here to visit me with genuine concern about my well-being?"

She shifted in her seat uncomfortably again. "Well um, Anthony, you two *are* brothers, of course I'd want you to look out for each other."

"Well who looked out for me? Did you put any money in my commissary, did you visit me ONE time in all of my eight years here? Did you write me ONE letter to see how I was doing or if I were still alive? Huh, MOM?"

She bit down on both of her lips and I saw tears at the bridge of her oval eyes. I couldn't believe that for the first time, I could finally see the resemblance of my own eyes inside of hers. It disgusted me that I shared blood with this woman.

"Look Anthony, I'm sorry, I know I should've been here for you. I just, I was-"

I cut her off again, fuck that! No excuse could constitute her absence. Before I knew who she was, she already knew that I lacked a mother's love my whole life. All I could do was laugh and nod to refrain from saying shit that I really wanted to say.

"You know what? A whole lot of motherfuckers have been telling me they are sorry lately. Actions speaks a whooole lot louder than words. But listen…" I aimed my eyes directly into hers because I wanted her to feel what I was saying to her. "I don't hate you, I really don't. I just can't *fuck* with you. I've always respected you over the years because you used to come around when me and Lea were coming up. But-." I caught myself getting choked up when I mentioned Lea's name and I had to pause before I continued. It was a name I hadn't brought up in years because it was too painful. It was her betrayal that landed me there in the first place.

She must've saw the pain in my eyes because she seemed to be sympathizing. "Speaking of Lea, have you heard from her? I heard she's doing really bad Anthony, I tried to contact her but I can't find where she's living. I'm worried about her."

"Look, all I can do is pray for her, like I'm going to do for you. Like I said, I'm not mad at you. I stopped expecting anything from anyone years ago. Can't get disappointed if you don't put expectations on how someone should treat you, right? So again, I don't hate you, I just don't fuck with you?"

"Grudges aren't good for your soul Ant. If you can't forgive me, at least forgive Lea. You two are siblings. Do you ever think that you'll be able to find it in your heart to forgive her?"

"Listen to me clearly because these will be the last words you will EVER hear from me. I don't fuck with her and I damn sure don't fuck with you, *mom*." I ended, sarcastically.

I raised up from the table. "Yo' guard. This visit is over."

She bent her head down, the bangs on her short, brown wig were stuck to her forehead because she had been sweating the entire visit. I had no other words for her ass. Her visit wasn't sincere. She literally only visited me to ask me to look out for J-Boy like she didn't give birth to me too. I don't even think she cared about how I was doing. That shit was fucked up and a nigga like me refused to sit there for twenty more minutes of the fuckery. I'd rather be locked up in my cell.

After being escorted back, I did a lot of thinking before rec time. I knew that once I got out, I'd literally have to start over when it came to who I was letting into my circle. My family was non-existent and I just planned to do me and build from there.

"Yo' Ant, you coming out to rec?" My cellmate knocked me out of my zone.

"Yeah I'm coming out." I shook off my thoughts and headed out to clear my head. Lifting weights always seemed to keep me from overthinking.

"How was your visit? Ma told me she was coming to visit you." J-Boy asked while spotting me as I bench pressed 200 pound weights.

"Oh you knew she was coming up here to visit me huh? How many times did she visit *you* since you been locked up?"

"Shit, like every week." He confessed.

I pushed the weight up into his hands and had him lift it back onto the stand as I sat up. "Guess how many times she came to visit me while I was in here? NONE! And nigga, if you were never transferred here, she probably wouldn't have *ever* came to visit me at all."

"Come on Ant, don't do that."

"Don't do what? She came up here to ask me to look out for you. She didn't ask me how I was doing or none of that shit. That's *your* mom nigga. That lady ain't shit to me."

I stood up and walked off. My adrenaline was rushing and I didn't want to take my anger out on J-Boy because it wasn't his fault. I was just a damaged ass nigga.

"Well what else she talk about in the visit?" J-Boy followed behind me.

"Nothing important. She brought up my sister and I didn't want to talk about that shit either."

J-Boy got quiet and he looked away. Niggas knew how close Lea and I used to be and how her testifying against me earned her a spot on my cut off list for life. Then he cleared his throat. "Man, I been hearing that she ain't doing so good out there dog."

"Well nigga, that ain't my problem." I said.

For the rest of my time in prison, neither J-Boy nor Terror brought Lea up ever again. I'm sure they also wanted to know if I'd ever forgive her. To me, that was no one's concern but mine.

"Anthony Currington, it's release day!" The guard called out.

Anxiety sunk deeply into the core of my stomach. Shit was getting real, real fast! Freedom was so close, I could taste it. I was daydreaming about it as I allowed J-Boy and Terror to sort through my items to see if they wanted anything before I tossed it out. I didn't want to take anything that I acquired from prison outside with me unless I needed it. It was time for a fresh start. The only item from prison besides Ms. Antonia's letters that I was taking with me was the picture of my nephew my sister sent me years ago that I had creased in my hand. Secretly his picture helped me get by while I was in prison. Little man looked so much like me, and it wasn't his fault that my sister did the salty shit she had done. Just knowing that there was another lil' man with the last name Currington made me feel proud. It still hurt that my sister told me that he had been infected with the monster too. I could only hope that his health was in a better state than what I hear hers was.

"Take care out there my nigga, I love you dog. Hold shit down for all of us. We ain't gonna' be in this bitch forever." Terror smiled with his hands up.

"Fuckin' right. Y'all will be out of this bitch soon enough." I agreed. I'd hope that my words would give them hope. I knew the feeling of only having hope to keep a nigga feeling free while being in prison. They had mad time still over their heads but whatever hope that they had, they needed to hold on to it to get them through.

"Love you bro. Feel like I'm saying goodbye." J-Boy said.

We locked eyes, I really think my nigga was about to cry. "Nigga, this ain't goodbye, this is till we meet again."

"Shit Ant, we all tried to be some low-key niggas out there, but truth be told, at the core of it all, we were all some thug ass niggas from Boston that didn't know any better. We were all tryna' make money and stunt on everybody in the hood. Except for you, you always saw a different vision. I sometimes sit back and wish that I was smart enough to listen to your wisdom. I was living fast, so death or jail was always lurking at every corner with that type of lifestyle I was living. You were like a father figure to all of us but now we just got to learn from our mistakes and chuck this prison shit up as part of the game. I know this may not mean anything to you but take Ma coming to visit you as a compliment. She knows how much we all look up to you, that's why she asked you to look out for me. She got love for you Ant, we all do."

"I hear you." I said.

"No, I'm serious. I appreciate everything you've done for me. And just know, prison can't hold some real niggas down forever." J-Boy pat his heart with his fist.

This was the first time that he had ever exposed his heart to me. Niggas was always too tough to talk about how they really felt because niggas thought expressing themselves to each other was gay. But I appreciated his vulnerability. I could only hope that from this day forward, he'd take heed to my guidance and do better once he got out.

"I won't let this prison shit kill me. I'm gonna' eat this time and we are going to be a crew again when I get out."

"This shit won't kill you, you're a strong ass nigga and we've been through a lot. Shit, a nigga like me don't even fear death anymore my nigga, I'll get to see my pops again."

"A'ight break all this sentimental shit up. We don't even need to talk about death, ain't none of us seeing the grave anytime soon my nigga, we got a lot to live for." Terror interrupted. "See you when we get out Ant, hold it down out there." He said.

"Anthony Currington, let's GO!" The guard pitched louder.

"Alright I love y'all, stay up. Brothers for life."

"Brothers for life." J-Boy and Terror repeated.

I walked out of the door and headed off to my new chapter.

Chapter 16

"Hola' Anthony." Nicky's mom, Ms. Antonia greeted me outside of the prison gates. She was leaning against her gray Ford Fusion smiling. Ms. Antonia was short, she stood about 4'11 and slender with thick, long brown hair. You could tell that in her youth, she really resembled Nicky.

She opened her arms and gave me the tightest hug.

"Hey, Ms. Antonia. You have no idea how much I appreciate this. "

"No problem. I told you I would help you. Now get in the car."

I laughed. Ms. Antonia was just as demanding as she was in the letters that she would send me. But it was innocent, she meant no harm.

She made her way to the driver's side and I opened the passenger door to let myself in. I hadn't been inside of a car in so long, it felt awkward. Freedom was definitely something I was going to have to get used to again.

"How do you feel Papitho? You are out of prison." She said rolling the" r" in the word prison. She spoke so fast and her Spanish accent was so thick, it was hard for me to keep up.

"I feel good, just ready to get myself together."

"You'll be fine Papitho." She said pulling away from the prison.

I glimpsed back at the shit-nest that I lived in for the past eight years of my life. I was happy to be out of there but I was unable to force a smile. I left many good niggas whom I built relationships with in there. I met some really good dudes that were doing life that would never be able to see the roads that I was now riding on ever again.

I sat back in my seat and closed my eyes to say thank you to GOD for allowing me to get through my bid unscathed.

"Papitho, reach for that bag by your foot." She instructed while driving. I sat up and reached for the bag she was referring to.

"I brought you a teléfono until you can buy yourself one."

I opened the box. "Wow, this is a good look, thank you Ms. Antonia. You really didn't have to do this."

"Nonsense, hush your boca, I'm going to help you. My daughter would've wanted me to do this."

Ms. Antonia was making a nigga feel supported. I know the phone she purchased for me was cheap because it was inside of a Walgreens bag, but I gave no fucks. It was only temporary until I was able to rebuild and I was thankful.

Finally we were in the hood and I was starting to really feel free now. These were the streets that me and the crew used to roam when we were youngings and as young adults getting money. I noticed some of the projects were turned into townhomes and the plots where there were once empty land were now turned into commercial buildings. I almost didn't recognize my own hood. But as much as they tried to make it look modern, the townhomes as well as the new buildings were riddled with graffiti and some of the old heads that were hanging out on the corners before I got locked up, were still out there. The scene had changed but everyone in the hood were doing the same ole' thing.

"Ms. Antonia, do you mind stopping by Joe's sub shop, that's the food place that I wrote you about. I been dreaming about a steak and cheese sub from Joe's for eight years. Is it still there?"

"Si, Joe's was renovated but it's still there, I'll take you there Papitho."

I told myself that my first meal out of prison would be a steak and cheese sub. Me and my sister used to tear up Joe's sub shop in

Dudley. Eating a bomb ass steak-and-cheese was going to bring back memories of how we used to enjoy moments together when pops was alive. However, I'd soon find that reminiscing on these memories were useless once we drew nearer to Joe's pizza shop. I saw a face that I hadn't seen it what seemed like forever.

"Stop the car Ms. Antonia!"

"Anthony, you trying to get us killed, this is Blue Hill Avenue, traffic is crazy."

"Pull over real quick, hurry up!" I pointed to an empty spot on the curb.

With precision, Ms. Antonia swayed her small car through the traffic toward the curb. I hopped out and headed towards the bus stop where I saw Lea sitting, appearing to be out of it. A young boy was sitting beside her and my nerves were on ten as I got closer.

"Lea?" I called out. My heart was fluttering, I never wanted to ever see her again but I felt compelled to confront her.

Slowly, she lifted her head in my direction. I didn't know rather to be angry or feel sorry for her. Lea looked awful. Her skin had darkened to almost a dark purple, her once 145 pound frame was slimmed down to about 119. Her eyelids were darker than her skin and they were baggy like mini blinds. Her ponytail was matted to her head as if it hadn't been combed in months and her one piece beige jumpsuit looked like it was turning gray.

"What happened to you?" I asked. As much anger that I had for her, I actually wanted to hug her and help her. I would've never expected to see my sister letting herself go this way. I was in total disbelief because she looked like a different person.

"How do you know my mommy?" The brown eyed lil' boy was protective of his mom. He stood up from the bus stop bench and demanded that I answer him.

173

I smiled to fight back my tears. "I'm your Uncle Anthony." I said.

"Uncle Anthony?" He repeated as if my name was familiar to him.

"Anthony?" Lea interrupted, crying once she realized that it was indeed me. Tears wasted no time drawing out of her eyes. "Anthony? My brother, Anthony." She walked towards me and in mid-step she began coughing uncontrollably. Vomit soon followed and it appeared as if blood was included in whatever she had regurgitated.

"Mom, mommy?" My nephew was crying out, patting her back. It was apparent that he was scared. He cried dramatically as he tried to lift my sister up who was now leaning on the bus stop post throwing up.

"Is the señora okay? I'm calling the ambulance." Ms. Antonia said as she crept up behind me.

"Yes, call the ambulance!" I shouted.

"Come on lil' man, come with uncle Ant, your mom is going to be fine." I assured him.

Surprisingly, minutes later, the ambulance arrived. They placed Lea on a stretcher and transported her to Boston Medical Center. Ms. Antonia and I took my nephew with us and we followed behind it. I hadn't been out a full day and things had already went left.

I turned to make sure my nephew's seatbelt was on and it was. Then I tried to calm him down because he was sitting quietly, crying. He was worried about his mom and obviously scared because he was in the car with two strangers who he had just met for the first time. "Lil' man, what's your name?"

"Everyone calls me little Ant." He said wiping his tears with his hands.

I smiled. "We have the same name little Ant."

"I know, mom says she named me Anthony because I reminded her of you and she thought that she would never see you again."

"Is that what she told you lil' man?"

"Yup, she said that you and my grandpa were the only ones who ever really loved her but I tell mom all the time that I love her too."

I smiled. He was smart as shit and his energy was dope. "I can see why she would name you after me. We definitely have the same heart. I can't wait to get to know you. Your mom is going to be okay, alright."

"I can't wait to get to know you too Uncle Ant? If my mom isn't okay, will you take care of me?" He asked.

A tight knot formed in my throat. I remembered the letter my sister wrote me stating how my nephew had been born with HIV. He was so handsome and he had so much promise in his eyes. His fate was beyond his control and he had to grow up in this cold world without the odds in his favor.

"I will always make sure you are taken care of, you hear me. I promise."

"Okay. Get out right here Papitho, I will park and bring the niño inside. We will find you. Go! Go now!" Ms. Antonia rushed me.

I hopped out the car and headed into the hospital to find my sister. I spotted one of her homegirls that I knew from back in the days named Laura. She was crying and standing at the front desk pulling tissues out of a Kleenex box.

"Laura, you know where Lea is?"

"Anthony? Oh my goodness, I can't believe that's you." She squeezed the Kleenex into her palms and rushed over to hug me tight.

"Yeah, I just got out today. I saw Lea at the bus stop and she started throwing up and shit. She looked bad, so we called an ambulance for her."

Laura nodded. "I work here Ant, I'm a nurse now.

I scoped out her blue scrubs. I was surprised because back in the day Laura was a straight hood rat. It was good to see that she got her shit together. She looked amazing.

"I see your sister in here all the time because she refuses to take her medicine. She's killing herself Ant." Laura stretched the tissue out of her palm and wiped her eyes with it because she started crying again.

"Why is she not taking her medication?" I was confused.

"She said that besides lil' Ant, she has nothing to live for. She makes sure lil' Ant stays on his medication religiously but she straight let herself go Anthony and I can't take watching my friend die. I keep trying everything I can to help her out but her T-cells are out of control. I keep telling her that if her CD4 count drops below 200 due to advanced HIV disease, she can be diagnosed with AIDS."

Feeling my head spinning, my emotions began to run high. Although we were estranged, it hurt me to see my sister in this state. "You're a nurse though, it makes no sense why you can't make her get her shit together."

"I try all the time Ant. I'm literally all that she has and I be begging her to take her medication. She lost you and your father and no one from the hood fucks with her because of what she did to you, so she's depressed. She's known as a snitch that got the monster, how would you feel? She has never forgiven herself for betraying you. I low-key think she's punishing herself for losing you."

I was at a loss for words. I mean, I heard people telling me how bad my sister was doing out here, but I had no idea that she was imposing it on herself.

176

"Take me to her room." I demanded.

Laura smudged her eyeliner and mascara onto her tissue as she curled her finger for me to follow her.

My stomach dropped as I walked inside of the hospital room where my little sister lay. It was evident that she was suffering. This bitch ass disease was eating her alive from the inside out. She bent her head in my direction and her eyes froze wide open when she saw me.

"She's sedated Anthony. Try to talk to her while she's still awake. I'll leave you in here to speak to her alone. I'm sure y'all have some catching up to do." Laura sniffed and walked out of the room leaving Lea and I alone together for the first time in eight years.

A tear slid down the side of Lea's cheek. "I'm sorry Anthony. I'm sorry, I'm so sorry." She started coughing again.

"Shhh. Don't talk. Just rest." I told her. She took a deep breath and her coughing subsided.

"You need to start taking your medication Lea. You have a son now that needs you. What would pops say about you just giving up and letting yourself go? Doesn't matter how *he* died, he wouldn't have wanted the same for you. There are plenty of people walking around living healthy with HIV."

"I don't want to live anymore Ant. If it wasn't for my son, I would've taken my life a long time ago. I'm lonely, I'm sick, I'm always in pain and Anthony, I'm soooo ugly." She cried and coughed heavily again.

I took her hand and squeezed it tight as she turned her head away trying to control her coughing. I watched upon her as she suffered from this illness that was dominating her body. She tried to face me again but she was still coughing and crying. "Take a deep breath and relax Lea." I took an overview of her face. Through her darkened skin, I still saw my pretty little sister who I loved so much. She had a son to raise and I needed her to get her shit together.

"Listen. You are still just as beautiful as you were when we were little." I couldn't fight back my tears any longer, my stubborn walls fell loose and I let it all out. I loved my little sister so much and it killed me to watch her suffering, even though I was still hurt by her betrayal. "Why did you do this shit to me Lea? You know I'd lay my life down for you! All this hustling and bullshit I was doing out here was for *you*! And all it took was for a nigga, a fuckin' outsider, to come into your life for you to betray me?"

"I know. I'm sorry, I'm going to be sorry till my last breath, brother."

"You ain't taking your last breath anytime soon sis. Your bro is home now, and I forgive you." I let forgiveness fall from my lips and when I spoke it, I let it come from my heart.

Lea smiled and turned her head, sinking it deeper into her pillow crying.

I turned her head back towards me. "You hear me little sis, I forgive you." I said really meaning it.

Her gaze into my eyes was confirmation that she had accepted my apology. Then she smiled and fought to stay awake. "You know I still have the big body TV at my house that pops had since we were little."

Immediately I wiped my face and got serious. My adrenaline rushed with intensity, this was music to my ears. "Lea listen to me, where's the TV?" I asked her anxiously. Her eyes slowly shut and she was unable to stay awake. She drifted off to sleep leaving me with unanswered questions.

"Damn!" I said, turning away from her bed. It was crazy, because after all this time, I thought that I'd have to count my winnings as losses, but Lea had just assured me that my bag was still secure. See, I had hidden most of the money I had made on the streets inside of that TV. It was my insurance in case something happened to me, that Lea would be straight. After she snitched on me, I thought she'd just take my money and run if she knew where it was so I never told her about it. As fate would have it, eight years later, I'm out of prison and about to relinquish money that was now needed to take care of lil' Ant. I lifted my head up to the ceiling, I swear pops was an angel looking out for me. He was probably proud of me for forgiving Lea and the reward was being able to have access to my bag again. I whispered, a quick thank you and fell back into my thoughts. Now I just needed to find my way to it. I glanced back at Lea who seemed to be sleeping good and I knew that my forgiveness made her feel at peace.

Chapter 17

I heard Ms. Antonia cursing in Spanish down the hallway in the hospital. She seemed to be frustrated that she was unable to locate me. "I'm looking for Anthony, ju' don't need to be rude, his sister was in the ambulance. Which room, tell me now?" She demanded.

"Listen, I don't know who you are talking about, you're going to have to calm down. I definitely don't want any problems from you Ms. Antonia but I just don't' know who you are talking about." The big burley security guard tried reasoning with her. He looked like he was an ex-gangster that was fortunate to get a job as security.

I charged toward their direction and lil' Ant spotted me first. "Uncle Anthony, is my mom okay?"

"She's fine, she's resting right now." Ms. Antonia cut her eyes at the security guard she was fussing at, she was so feisty, she looked like she wanted to set it off on him. I had to calm her ass down and keep the peace. Last thing I needed was to get into it with a security guard, my first day home.

"My fault, she was looking for me." I told the guard.

He lifted his hands up. "I just don't want any trouble up here. We don't need that type of drama here." The security guard said exalting his authority, but seeming as if he knew Ms. Antonia.

"Ain't no drama. She's good." I said trying to calm the situation down again. Ms. Antonia was on her Griselda Blanco shit and it seemed like she had homey shook. As far as I was concerned, it definitely wasn't that serious. I took Ms. Antonia's hand and led her to some padded chairs in the hospital. Clearing my mind was all that I wanted to do. I sat and rubbed my hand over my face. "I'm sorry Ms. Antonia, I didn't mean to keep you waiting; I just needed to have some words with my sister."

"Is she going to be okay?" She asked.

"Yeah, I think she needed to know that I forgave her so that she could forgive herself."

"I understand." She said.

Suddenly I spotted Laura walking toward Lea's room. "Laura, come here real quick." I shot up to catch up to her.

"Ant, how'd it go in there?" She asked seeming concerned.

"I mean, I spoke to her and I told her I forgave her. I think she's going to be okay from now on."

Laura basically hopped into my arms. She hugged me so tightly, I could feel her nails through my jacket. "Thank you Anthony, she needed that. She's been suffering and punishing herself for so long, GOD Bless you Ant."

"Thanks." I said. I peeked back and saw my nephew sitting next to Ms. Antonia playing with a small toy that he retrieved from his pocket. That's when I realized that I needed to get him to somewhere safe. This was my first day back home, I was just securing a place to stay for myself; I didn't know what I was going to do with a child.

"Laura, you think you can keep my nephew until my sister recovers?" I asked her.

She nodded. "I don't know Ant. I have a son myself and I already have problems with getting sitters for him because they are so expensive. I can probably keep him for a week tops." She tilted her heads towards Lea's room and I saw two people walking inside.

"I actually called someone here to visit Lea. I've been calling them every time she gets sick. Once she recovers, they disappear again but at least a small amount of support is better than none, right? I think you should go have a conversation with them yourself. I'll stay out here with lil' Ant till you're done."

Laura sat next to Ms. Antonia, introduced herself and started playing with lil' Anthony. I made steps toward Lea's room wondering who could be visiting her. Today was getting more eventful by the minute.

I took slow treads into the room. There was a woman and man standing over Lea and the woman was rubbing her head.

"Hey?" I called out.

They both turned my way at the same time. Within minutes I noticed that it was the woman who I thought was my mom my whole life. Still beautiful and youthful as if she hadn't aged a bit since I've been locked up. She still resembled the singer Aaliyah but she aged like Beyonce's mom, Tina Knowles.

"What are you doing here?" I asked her.

She gasped. "Anthony?" The shocked expression that laced her face was as if she'd seen a ghost. She forced an abrupt hug and just like the last time I had saw her, I didn't hug her back. I couldn't. Out of respect, her husband cleared his throat and stepped out of the room to give us privacy. He did the right thing but I had no words for this woman. She had lied to me my whole life.

"You look great. I see you grew out a beard like your dad had. You look just like him." She said to me as she sniffed and scoped me out from head to toe. The dim lighting in the room filtered onto her face, exposing her tears which drained from her eyes effortlessly. I'm sure she felt guilty for not being there for me.

"I don't have nothing to say to you." I told her.

She licked her lips and took in a healthy breath. It seemed like she was searching for the right words to say next.

"That's fair. Well, I heard that you found out the truth about your mom. I always wanted to be the one to tell you. To me, I will always be your mom." She placed both her hands to her heart.

"Just stop it. Neither one of you deserve that title. You say that you will always be my mom but wouldn't a mom had visited me in prison?"

Lea let out two hard gasps and we turned toward the bed. I rushed to the opposite side of her to take her hand and my fake ass mom held Lea's hand from the side she was standing. We both watched on Lea with heavy hearts without saying a word. I still loved my sister and I just wanted her healthy and I'm sure my so-called mom wanted the same for her.

I lifted my head to speak to her. "You never did anything for us our entire lives. You didn't raise us, you lied to us, abandoned us, and left a gaping hole in our hearts that could never be repaired. If you could just fulfill one thing for me, and I will never ask you for anything else in life." I gathered myself before finishing my request because I wanted her to know that I was serious, and I took in a deep breath. "Just make sure that lil' Anthony is straight and always will be."

She released her hand from Lea's and reached for mine. Reluctantly I met her hand halfway and she squeezed it tight. "Consider it done Anthony, I promise." She said with sincerity in her moist eyes.

She left me with her phone number and I exited the room and found myself back to the waiting area.

Laura stood up. "Everything go okay?" She asked.

"Yeah, everything's straight." I told her.

"That's good to hear Anthony." She smiled. "Well, I got lil' Ant for the week, don't worry about him. I'm going to try my best to make sure he's good. He has all his meds in his little backpack, so he'll be fine." Laura assured me.

"Okay cool, good looking out. I really appreciate it." I said feeling relieved. Laura and I exchanged phone numbers and I bent down to say goodbye to lil' Ant. "You were real brave today. You remind me of me, protective of your mom and a heart full of gold. Don't ever lose those qualities, you hear me?"

He smiled. "I hear you Uncle Ant, I want to be just like you when I grow up." He said with pride. I felt a rock stuck in my throat as I tried clearing it to force out my next words. Just knowing that there was a possibility that this disease could defeat him before he became an adult had my head fucked up. He didn't deserve that shit. "You are going to be waaaay better than me. You hear me?"

"I hear you Uncle." He smiled.

"Has your mom ever told you about your grandfather?"

"Yes." He answered.

"He would've loved you." I said wishing pops could see how dope his grandson was.

"I know." He said with confidence. Ms. Antonia and Laura and I all laughed. Lil' Ant was indeed one of a kind. I pecked my nephew on the cheek and told Laura that I'd be in touch with her ASAP. It was time for me to settle in at Ms. Antonia's so that I could find my way back to my money.

I watched as Laura took lil' Ant to see his mom so that he could say goodbye before she took him home. A small smile formed on my face watching the back of his curly head eager to see his mom. He was so brave, braver than I ever was.

"You ready Anthony?" Ms. Antonia asked. I broke out of my gaze and followed her outside to her car.

Chapter 18

I was hoping that Ms. Antonia lived in a laid back neighborhood but she lived smack dab in the hood. I mean, I knew that her crib was going to be temporary quarters for me but judging from the atmosphere, I was going to have to make moves ASAP. Crack heads riddled her street and niggas were on their porches smoking weed and mugging me when I got out of the car. I was hoping that no one would recognize who I was. I didn't want the streets to know that I was out of jail just yet. I wanted to be low-key for as long as possible.

Ms. Antonia twisted her key in her front door and held it open for me. The smell was the first thing that I noticed. The aroma of Spanish food was prevalent and since I never got a chance to pick up my steak-and-cheese sub, the yellow rice and beans with pollo smelled like life! It reminded me of the good food that Nicky used to cook for me.

"Come! This is your room." Ms. Antonia led me down a small hallway. I took a quick peek into the first room on my right where I noticed it was full of pictures of Nicky. It was sort of like Ms. Antonia made the room a full shrine dedicated to Nicky. I got butterflies in my stomach; I swear I felt Nicky's calming presence coming from that room.

"There's clean linen on the bed, I bought you T-shirts, boxers and socks, they are all in the drawer. I didn't know what size sweatpants that ju' wear so I got ju' an X-L."

A nigga was so grateful, I wanted to hug Ms. Antonia so badly. And I surprised myself when I did. I think I caught her off guard as well but I was pleased when she slowly hugged me back. I was never the affectionate type of nigga but I was truly grateful that she was showing me how a mother was supposed to treat a child. Maybe I was just desperate for a mother's love, or any type of love for that matter, but a nigga was just grateful.

"I'm so sorry. I know I caught you off guard Ms. Antonia. I just never had someone treat me like this. No mother figure was ever really in my life. I was always the one holding everyone around me down. I appreciate you, from the bottom of my heart." I pat my chest.

"Anthony, don't apologize." She placed her hand on my right cheek and she peered into my eyes briefly almost as if she was trying to read me. "You are a good guy, I can tell you have a great heart. I see why Nicky was so into you. I wish you were able to help her get in control of her addiction. I really miss her." She turned away.

"Man, I miss her too." I said as we shared a moment. Ms. Antonia grew a bit more sentimental and rushed out of the room. I guess she didn't want me to see her in that state so I respected her privacy. I collected a wash cloth and a towel off of the bed and navigated through the apartment to find the bathroom. I twisted the shower on and began feeling anxiety. This was my first shower as a free man and I felt so Blessed to be able to be standing in this moment. I allowed the hot water to fall onto my face as I began to release tears. I thought about pops, Lea, my lil' nephew and my baby Nicky. I felt an overwhelming feeling of her presence right next to me, cheering me on. I remember one of the old heads in jail told me that love, real love only entered your life once in your lifetime. The way that Nicky loved me was so pure and so effortless, and if her love was the only love that this lifetime had to offer me, I was fine with that because I enjoyed every moment I was able to spend with her. And being around her mom felt incredible because it seemed as if Nicky was always there.

I turned off the shower, took my towel off the sink and found my way back to my room. I slipped on my boxers and T-shirt that Ms. Antonia had bought me and I met her in the kitchen.

"Eat your food before it gets cold." She demanded. Her bossy vibes were on a hunnet but I was beginning to get used to it.

"Thank you. I'm about to tear this food up." I slipped into the kitchen chair and picked up my fork.

"Eat up Papitho, I know you're hungry." She poured me some lemonade and I drank it like it was keeping me alive. This meal and that lemonade was pure magic. I must've eaten the whole pan of chicken and half the large pot of rice and it cracked Ms. Antonia up. She laughed as I demolished the food because every time I refilled my plate, I demolished it like a damn pig.

Finding her way to a bottle of red wine in the kitchen, she poured herself a glass and fell asleep on the couch. I pulled a blanket that I found on the love seat and laid it on Ms. Antonia so that she'd be comfortable. I made my way back to my bed so that I could strategize. First person I called was Laura. I checked to see if lil' Ant was okay first and she said that he and her son were both sound asleep.

"I have to ask you a question Laura. Do you know where my sister lives?" I asked her.

"Yeah, of course." She answered.

"Well I need to get over there to get something. Do you have the key?"

"Yes, I have Lea's purse with me."

"Perfect!" I said relieved. "You think you can pick me up tomorrow afternoon and bring me over there?" I asked her.

"Um, I gotta' work until 3 o'clock tomorrow Ant."

"Okay bet, I'll have someone take me to try to get my license and shit straightened out and all the other bullshit I have to catch up on since I've been locked up, then I'll link up with you after."

"Okay, that works." She said before hanging up.

I reached over to my jail bag and retrieved Lim and Rico's numbers. They had been out for a quick sec now and I know they'd been dying to hear from me.

I called Rico first. "Who's this?" He answered.

"It's Ant nigga!"

"Ant money, fuck is good my nigga, you home?" His tone lingered with excitement.

"Nigga, I'm fresh the fuck out!"

"My nigga's HOME!!!" He shouted through the phone. The feeling was refreshing to know that we carried our bond outside of prison.

"What's good with Lim?" I asked him.

"Yo', that nigga's right here, hold up, I'm about to put you on speaker."

"That nigga Ant!" Lim called out.

"What up nigga! Y'all niggas are free and already out here on your bullshit, huh?"

"Nigga hellllll no! We keeping our nose clean. I ain't never going back to that bitch!" Lim said.

"Yo', Ant, I got some bad bitches coming over in a few, want us to come scoop you?"

As tempting as pussy sounded, that was furthest thing from my mind. I just needed these niggas to hold me down so that I could get to my bag, after that, then I would think about having some fun. While I was in prison, I made a promise to myself that when I got out, my priorities would be in order so I wasn't with the shits right now.

"Nah', I just need one of y'all niggas to pick me up tomorrow so I can go to the DMV and see what's good with my license and shit."

"My shits all fucked up." Rico said. "Mine too, I gotta' pay like three bands to get mine back." Lim said.

I laughed. "I got something for that." I told them. Little did they know, the bag that I was about to collect, would change all of our lives overnight, but I was determined to move smart.

"My sister been pushing us around, text me the address and we'll come scoop you tomorrow." Rico said.

"A'ight got you. And don't forgot to lock this number in, this is my new cell."

"Bet." Rico said.

I hung up the phone, got comfortable in the full size bed and spent my first day out of prison sleeping comfortably, knowing that I was going to be able to help my people work towards a more solid future.

Chapter 19

Ms. Antonia was real nosy when Lim and Rico picked me up. I saw her watch from the cracked blinds as I got into the car to scope out who I was with. I figured that she felt a bit left out that I had other people helping me out so I knew that I'd have to do something to make her feel special when I got back.

Rico's sister was a straight square, you could tell that she didn't grow up in the hood and she wasn't playing no games when it came to disrespect or not following the rules. She made it clear that her brother would not be driving her car until his license was straight.

"This is my sister Selena." Rico introduced.

"Nice to meet you." I said shaking her hand before she pulled off from the street. Although she was black and Spanish like Rico and Lim, she looked like she was a hundred percent Spanish. Pretty yellow skin and jet black, long, crinkly hair. Her accent was heavy but her speech was also proper.

"What's good nigga!" Lim and Rico both faced me as Selena headed towards the registry. "Man, it just feels good to be home." I said sinking into my seat. Lim and Rico had fresh haircuts and new white T-shirts on. They looked like brand new niggas and almost resembled each other. They both looked similar to that Rapper Dave East.

"Yo' I couldn't take looking at another nigga for another day. I don't see how niggas could do life and never be able to see pussy again." Rico said loudly.

"Watch your mouth!" Rico's sister hit his shoulder.

"I forgot Mother Theresa was in here and shit." Rico laughed.

"So listen, y'all niggas got any plans for opening businesses and setting up some of the shit we were talking about when we were locked up?" I asked them.

"Man, I got an interview at this Construction Company and shit but they only pay $12.00 an hour. A nigga' gonna' end up slangin' some shit on the side if I got to work for them fuckin' pennies." Lim said.

"I ain't got shit lined up and I ain't lookin'. When I need some doe, I know how to get it. My nigga's set me up with a lil' something that should last me for a few months." Rico revealed.

"That's that small-minded thinking. I'm talking about being your own boss, opening businesses you can leave for your family. A legacy." I explained.

Lim and Rico both looked at each other dumbfounded. All I could do was shake my head. I had hoped that all the talk about opening businesses and shit when we were locked up, wasn't just some jail talk. But niggas just be saying anything when they are locked up because it sounds good. As soon as they smelled freedom, nigga's be right back to doing what they did to get themselves locked up.

Rico's sister pulled up to the registry and found a parking spot in the lot. She placed the car in park and unlocked the doors. "I'm going to run into Dunkin Donuts, it's right next door." She said reaching for her purse beside me and Lim in the back seat and leaving the car. She left us alone at what I felt like was the right moment. This was my last chance to get their minds right. They had so much promise in them, but they didn't realize their potential. Lim and Rico reminded me of J-Boy and Terror and I didn't want them to drift off in the wrong direction like they did so I was determined for them to hear me out.

"Listen, I need to talk to y'all." Lim and Rico were both all ears. The car was quiet, we were all fresh out of prison and I felt like the timing was perfect. "I had some shit put up while I was away and I'm about to get to my bag real soon. I plan to wash the money by opening up a car dealership. Rico, your sister seems like she's good money, we can have her working there and other family members if you trust them. We can keep the money within the community and inside our families so we don't have to do no dumb shit out here."

"Car dealership? I don't know nothing about that shit. If you got a bag, let's go cop some work." Lim said proudly.

"See, that's that fuck-boy talk my nigga. We grown, you got locked up trying to get money for your seed thinking that way. You're a father now nigga, someone is depending on you. What would your seed say if you were back on the streets selling work again? You think he'll be proud of his pops? You gotta' be smart my nigga." I pressed my temple to emphasize my last thought.

"I'm listening, I just don't know if this shit will work. I'm kinda' with Lim on this one homey, we can cop some work and flip whatever you got." The both dapped each other up and laughed naively.

I grew frustrated. "Y'all see where my niggas J-Boy and Terror are right now, right? The same shitty ass place we were just living at for years out of our lives. That shits for basic niggas. We are Kings!"

"Nigga, we just some niggas from the hood, that King shit niggas be spitting is overrated." Rico stated.

"With that small time nigga-mentality, that's all y'all both are going to be, is just some niggas from the hood."

I left them both to sit with my last words as I let myself out of the car. Rico's sister was walking by me sipping an iced coffee. "You seem different from them, don't get wrapped up in their world, I love Lim and Rico, but they are going nowhere fast." She said nodding and walking to the car.

I digested her words with an open mind. I had different expectations for Lim and Rico but I was too old to be helping grown men become men. I had my own family to look after. I had hoped that my talk with them would get their minds on the right track, but only time would tell.

Luckily I didn't have to sit in the registry all day. My number was called within ten minutes and an African female clerk full of attitude as if she didn't like her job was helping me. She handed me a list full of tickets and fines from cars that I hadn't driven since I'd been locked up. With attitude dripping in her tone, she explained that I had to pay to have all of my tickets and fines expunged from my record before I was able to get my license back. I wasn't worried, I had plenty of money to pay them off, I just needed to get to it first.

I hopped back in the car and Selena asked if I was finished handling my business.

"Yeah, I'm good." I told her.

My ride back to Ms. Antonia's crib was spent thinking. Lim and Rico was loud as fuck talking about all types of irrelevant shit that didn't have anything to do with bettering themselves. So I tuned them out. They both still had that small-minded, hood mentality and I hoped that my ways would rub off on them so that they'd see the bigger picture soon.

I stared hard at them both before exiting the car. "Yo! Think about what I said to y'all. Get y'alls minds right and hit me later."

"A'ight my nigga." Rico reached back to dap my hand and Lim reached his out and did the same. I walked up to Ms. Antonia's crib and I knocked on the door. She answered it with her arms folded and a cigarette nudged in between her lips. I smiled at her because I knew that my little surprise would make her smile. Before I came, I had Selena stop by Joe's sub shop so that I could pick up a sub for me and Ms. Antonia. I told her that I wanted her to taste the sub I kept bragging about.

"I got something for you?" I smiled, placing the bag with the subs on the table.

"What ju' got for me?" She asked.

193

I pulled the sub out of the bag and opened the wrapping for her.

"This is a steak and cheese from Joe's, I told you how good they were. Remember when I wrote you and told you how I couldn't wait to taste one when I got out?"

Finally she let her guard down. I don't know why she was being so tough but I was hoping to soften her up. I thought maybe it was because I was still a stranger no matter how many letters we wrote each other and she wanted more communication with me when I left the house.

Ms. Antonia put out her cigarette, poured herself a glass of wine and then sat with me at the table. She picked up half of the sub and took a bite. "Mmmm. Delicioso!" She formed an 'okay' with her fingers.

"See, I told you." I laughed. Ms. Antonia tore that sub up. While eating it, she went on and on about how good it was. She spoke about the onions down to the seasoning. We laughed together and shared more memories of Nicky and she was really starting to let her defenses down.

"You are a really good man Anthony. I can't believe your mother missed out on the opportunity to raise such a gentleman."

Her words caught me off guard. All I could say was thank you. I felt uncomfortable when it came to talking about feelings, especially feelings associated with my mom.

Bzzz! Bzzz! My phone began vibrating on the table. This was music to my ears because I'd be able to escape talking about mushy shit with Ms. Antonia.

"Hello?" I answered.

"Hey Ant, it's Laura, I'll be there in about ten minutes, is that cool?" She asked.

"Oh, yeah, that's fine." I told her. I had almost forgot that I had texted her Ms. Antonia's address the day before. I pressed end and explained to Ms. Antonia that I'd be back later.

Laura literally arrived ten minutes later and once again Ms. Antonia was looking at us through the blinds as if she was a nosy neighbor.

"Who's that lady you are staying with Ant? She looked familiar at the hospital." Laura asked, taking a rubber band off of her wrist to throw her shoulder length black and blonde streaked hair into a ponytail.

"She's my ex's mom."

"Ooooh, Nicky's mom? I heard she took it hard when Nicky died. Shit, I heard that lady was crazy."

"Watch your mouth." I immediately checked Laura. Being disrespectful in regards to Ms. Antonia after she opened her doors and looked out for me was a no-no.

"I'm sorry Ant, I'm just telling you what I heard."

I changed the subject. "How's lil' Ant?" I asked her.

"Oh he's good, he plays really well with my son. He's so well behaved, I never have issues out of him."

"Where's he at now? I asked her.

"They are both with a sitter at my house, he's fine." She assured me.

After about fifteen minutes, she pulled up to the back of a gray duplex. The siding was run down and the parking lot was unsightly. Trash was everywhere and it smelled like a dead body.

"This is where she had my nephew staying? This shit got to change." I said stepping over all of the empty soda bottles and chicken bones following Laura to the door.

"Yeah, it's definitely dirty over here but living next to Forest Hills Station is much better than living closer to the hood." She said arming through her purse for the keys.

Finally she opened the door and I was beyond disappointed in my sister's living conditions. The entire environment was toxic. From the mold on the kitchen tile, old food rotting on the cabinets and clothes sprinkled everywhere. It looked like it had been abandoned for years.

"Oh yeah, my nephew is getting the fuck out of here!" I said blowing the dirt that was caked up on the coffee table. I turned toward a hidden corner in the living room that was blocked off by a purple curtain. I pushed the curtain to the side and saw the big body TV that I remembered from my childhood. Painted memories of my family when we were happy and I wrestled to fight back my tears. First thing I noticed on top of the TV was the picture of me, Lea and pops. I realized that I must've been about the same age as lil' Ant was now and I took the picture off the TV to take with me. Sitting in a frame next to it was a picture of lil' Ant smiling bright. I took both photos and cuffed them under my arm. The people in the pictures meant way more to me than what was inside of the TV.

I felt Laura creeping up behind me. "What are you doing?" She asked.

"Hold these, I'm taking them with me." I said handing her the pictures.

She took the pictures from my hands and stepped to the side. I grabbed hold of the TV and slid it out of the corner.

"Are you trying to take the TV too?" Laura asked confused. "You know that won't fit in my car right?"

196

I clapped the dirt off my hands from pulling on the TV and made a split decision. Laura was out here holding my sister down more than anyone, if I couldn't trust her, then who could I trust?

"Can I trust you?" I asked her.

"Of course you can Ant, what's wrong?" Her pretty face was concerned.

I popped the back of the TV open and the dusty hundreds stacked in rubber bands fell to my feet.

"Oh my goodness Anthony! Where'd all that money come from?" She asked surprised.

I bent to pick up one of the stacks and flicked it. "No one knew this was here while I was locked up and I want it to remain that way. I'm using this shit to get my family out of here. I'm opening up some legit shit in the hood so that the money can stay in the community and I'm leaving Boston." I bent to grip another stack. "Here, use this for you and your son."

Laura cried. "Really Ant? I don't know what to say, I've been out here struggling so bad. Between student loans, rent, daycare and my Honda that breaks down every other week, I'm out here living paycheck to paycheck. I don't know how I could ever repay you." She said in tears.

I nodded. "You held my sister down when everyone gave up on her. You deserve it. And I don't know how you got that lady to start visiting her."

"That lady Ant? Lea told me that you and J-Boy had the same mom. But *that lady* still identifies herself as *your* mom too."

"Well she isn't. But regardless, I hope that one day she's apart of lil' Ant's life and make up for lost time. She owes me and Lea that much."

Laura grinned and shook her head. "You are amazing Anthony. I've always admired you. You're not just some clueless street nigga, to me you're a King, a leader, a provider. And you don't do it for show, you do it from your heart, and that's what makes you so real."

"I appreciate that." I spoke, humbly.

I picked up three stacks to take with me. I didn't want to keep too much cash at Ms. Antonia's crib, but shit, I didn't want to keep it at my sister's crib either. I needed Laura to hold me down.

"Listen, I want you to stop by here every other day to transport the money in small increments out of the TV and over to your crib. I need it to be somewhere safe."

"I got you Anthony." Laura replied sincerely. For some reason I really trusted her and I knew that my money would be just fine in her care.

The small amount that I took with me would help me pay to get my license in order, assist in paying off whatever debt Lim and Rico had and help them get on their feet while I started the process of building my company for everyone's future.

I quickly placed the rest of the money that fell out of the T.V back inside. I nestled the TV back into the corner behind the purple curtain. I found a black bag in Lea's living room to put my cash inside, Laura tucked hers inside of her black square purse and we left.

On the way back to Ms. Antonia's, it was like Laura was at a loss for words. The only words she kept spitting out was, "thank you." I don't think she grasped the fact that it was my pleasure to break her off for being there for my sister when no one else was. I respected her loyalty.

"Alright Laura, don't forget what I said. Move the money, little by little out of Lea's house into your crib, you said you live in Milton and have an alarm on your apartment, I'll feel much secure with it there. Thank you for holding me down. You're a real one." She grabbed my arm before I left the car. "No Anthony, you're a real one, I swear you are heaven sent. GOD Bless you." She said.

"GOD Bless you too." I spit back.

"Nicky was really lucky to have you." She said batting her long eyelashes sincerely.

I smiled. "No, I was lucky to have her. No other woman had love for a nigga the way she did. She was special." I opened the door and Laura stopped me again.

"Wait. One more thing Ant. What are you planning on doing with all that money?"

"I'm going to open up a car dealership. My pops loved cars, that's all he talked about when I was younger, driving cars that he couldn't afford. I think this will make me feel a little closer to him. I think he'd be proud that I'm keeping the money in the community while doing something he always wanted to do." I revealed.

Laura smiled. "Yeah, I remember Lea always telling me about how your father loved cars. He *would* be really proud of you Ant."

I reached over and hugged Laura goodbye. Her sweet strawberry scent grazed my nose and she held me tightly. I could feel through her hug how grateful she was for my help. Little did she know, I was more grateful for her help because she was sincere and since I've known her so long; she felt like family.

I exited the car and crept up to Ms. Antonia's door. I knocked lightly, I didn't have a set of keys made yet and I felt guilty that I had to wake her up.

She opened the door without saying a word.

"I'm sorry for waking you up." I whispered. She waved her hand and walked slowly back into her bedroom. When she shut her bedroom door, I heard the lighter spark and smelled the cigarette she had just lit.

I tried to make as little noise as possible when I got into my bedroom. I took off my shoes and grabbed two grand from my stack and I crept back into the kitchen area to place it there. As soon as I put it down and turned around, Ms. Antonia was standing there in the dark. The light from the cigarette helped light up her slender silhouette on the wall when she took a pull.

Finally she flicked on the kitchen light. "What are you doing?" She asked me.

"Nothing, I just wanted to leave this here for you."

She panned her eyes toward the money and accidently dropped the cigarette from her hand. I chuckled and picked it up for her. "Don't be shocked, it's okay, this money is for you, you deserve it." I said putting the cigarette out in a nearby ashtray.

Ms. Antonia broke out of her shock and gave me a strong hug. I was delighted to be able to make her life a little bit easier. I planned to do much more for her because to me, she deserved it.

"Thank you." She said.

"My pleasure." I assured her.

I heard my phone ringing from my bedroom.

"I'll be right back."

"Si, Papitho." She waved me off and grabbed the money off the table. She cradled it in her hand and went into her bedroom. Probably to count it.

I lifted up my phone from the bed to answer it. "Hello?" I answered.

Deep cries resounded through the speaker. "Hello?" I asked again, now recognizing Laura's cry.

"Anthony, it's Lea, the hospital just called me. They said that she's dying. They've done all that they could do but it's too late. Anthony, I can't take this, she can't be dying, I can't lose my friend Anthony."

"Listen Laura, calm down, okay? Let me figure something out."

"Anthony?" I heard her call out. But I ended the call and tossed my phone across the bed. Truth was, I didn't know what the fuck to do. I stood up and began to pace the room. The fact that this situation was beyond my control and that I couldn't fix it, made it sting that much more. I spotted the picture that I had taken from Lea's crib earlier. Tears congregated at my eyes as I stared at us as kids, with pops, smiling in the picture without a worry in the world. I really wished that we could go back to those times. I swear it felt like a dark cloud was over my head. The fact that no one that I've ever loved or who has ever had love for me, never stayed in my life permanently, was taxing on my spirit. In that moment, I knew that I needed a higher power to calm me down before I was ready to find my way to the hospital. Otherwise, I felt like I was about to snap!

I snatched the picture off the bed and headed to the room where Ms. Antonia had made the shrine of memories of Nicky. That particular room seemed as if it was spiritual and that if I prayed in there, God would listen. I was desperate and I needed for my prayers to be heard immediately. The house was quiet but when I crept passed Ms. Antonia's room, I heard her whispering and she was being feistier than usual.

"Listen to what I told your ass! I said forget it!" Her whisper was high and stern, then she started verbalizing in Spanish. I snuck by her room and shut the door behind me when I got to the shrine. A lighter was laying beside a white candle next to Nicky's picture and I used it to light it up. I placed my family's picture right beside Nicky's smiling face. I got down on my knees and squeezed my eyes shut and took a deep breath before I spoke.

"I can't handle anymore losses. I surrender, all the money, all my plans, I surrender everything to you right here, right now if you just let my sister live. Please! I've suffered enough; I don't have anything left in me." Suddenly I felt a cold chill, breeze against my skin and I swear I saw the flame of the candles start burning harder. I'm not sure if it was a sign or confirmation that my prayers were being heard. I closed my eyes again and I prayed harder than I had ever prayed. I needed GOD, I needed help, I needed healing. I was tired. But I also knew that whatever GOD's will was, would be done. A nigga was drained, stressed and worn out. The feeling of being alone was especially overwhelming now. Even more overwhelming then I felt when I was in prison. I raised up off my knees and spotted a picture on the dresser in the corner. That's when I really realized just how alone I really was. I lifted the picture off the dresser to examine it closer. Nicky was in the picture, she appeared to be about sixteen or seventeen, however the two familiar faces that stood out made my antennas shoot up. I darted out of the room to confront Ms. Antonia but I was met with a blunt force object aiming at my head.

BOOM!!!

I didn't even see it coming so there was no way that I could avoid it.

The butt of the gun slammed against my forehead and forced me down to the floor. Blood quickly swam from my head down into my eyes and my vision was blurry.

"Nooooo!!!" Ms. Antonia screamed. "I said forget it! I called it off!" She shouted louder. I slowly let go of the picture that I held in my hand which revealed Nicky standing next to Lim and Rico as teens. I didn't understand the connection until I heard the three of them arguing while hovering over me.

"You said you wanted him gone for getting Nicky addicted to those pills. Why do you want to back out now? You said he was the reason why Nicky's dead, Aunty Antonia! We been game facing this nigga for years in prison, you can't back out now, fuck that! It's now or never!" Rico yelled at Ms. Antonia but he still had a gun pointed in my direction and he was now holding it with both hands.

"I got to have the dumbest nephews in the world. I said DON'T shoot him! STOP!" Ms. Antonia demanded.

I saw Lim smirk. "Nah, don't shoot him just yet, what about that money he was talking about, we need that shit." Lim spit.

Laying there in disbelief, I managed to smile through my pain. If this was the way that I was going out, then I was going out with my dignity like a man. I would never let these niggas have the satisfaction of thinking some sucker shit like this would give them stripes. Lim stood near the bottom of my feet and squat so I could hear him.

"Where the fuck is this money you were telling us about nigga? You obviously ain't gonna' need it anymore." He said laughing. "And wipe that smile off your face nigga, ain't shit funny."

"Fuck you nigga!" When he stood to his feet, I kicked him in the shin with as much strength I could conjure up.

"Owww, motherfucker!" Both Lim and Rico started kicking me in my sides and my legs with their Timberlands boots on. Rico took it a step further and started stomping me in the chest and ribs. The concussion in my head had me so weak, I couldn't even feel their stomps or kicks. I felt like I was starting to fade out. Every time I attempted to try to get up, my body wouldn't let me.

"I said stop, he's a good person! Stop doing this!" Ms. Antonia kept screaming and pulling at her hair. But Lim and Rico showed no mercy. They asked me where the money was again, I spit out blood and said, "FUCK YOU!" And I chuckled again. The duo started kicking and stomping harder and all I could do was look up at the light on the ceiling. It was so calming and overwhelmingly peaceful. Flashes of my pops smiling appeared in my vision and then I saw a glimpse of Nicky. I heard her say, "I love you Anthony." And her lovely smiled appeared clear as day. Suddenly my immediate vision got clearer again and I managed to see Rico with the evilest mug cocking the gun back and pushing it into my forehead.

"Noooo!!" Ms. Antonia was screaming right beside him so loudly. But her cries were faint to me and almost completely mute.

"Fuck that money! This is for my cousin Nicky nigga!" I closed my eyes and I said a Prayer. It was as if I was having an inner monologue with myself. If this was my final moment, I wanted to be forgiven for all the bad that I had done. I wanted to exit with a clear conscious. I've lived a fast life and the odds were never really in my favor, but I never complained and always made due with the circumstances I was given. I can't front, this time I was totally blind-sided, but fuck it, I didn't regret a thing. I was loyal and stayed down for everyone around me. I never did shit just to fit in, I did it from my heart and I just hoped that's the way I'd be remembered. I really think God heard my prayer earlier, I told him that I was tired, so if this was the way that I was going out, then he agreed that I was. I mean how much more could a nigga take? I took one final breath as I looked in the eyes of the coward who I thought was my friend.

"I told you your special day was coming nigga!"

I smiled in his face. My conscious was clear and my heart was pure. Especially since I let go of all of the resentment I held against lea. I stayed loyal to everyone around me since day one and I wouldn't change any of the memories I shared with pops, Lea, Nicky, the crew and even Lim and Rico. Niggas was just lost and didn't know any better. I laid there remembering the only advice my real mom gave to me when she visited me in prison. She said, "Anthony, grudges aren't good for the soul." She was right. I coughed and then took one last look at Rico and said, "I forgive you."

He stood tall, aimed at my body and began to shoot!

POW!!!!!!

The sound of the gun shooting into my chest didn't seem real. I felt myself hemorrhaging and it felt like I was suffocating. I saw a peaceful light trying to force it's way through my sight. Nicky's smile was seen in the back of the light and she was waving for me to follow her. She was dressed in an all white flowy dress with white roses in her hair. I saw myself taking steps towards her, almost as if I was out of my body and then..... POW!!!!!! The second shot forced all of the air out of my body. I no longer felt anything. No more suffering, no more worrying, I was free.

"Whyyyyy did you do this! You are so stupid, whyyyyy!!! Ms. Antonia's voice resounded, as everything soon faded to black.

****

Chapter 20

Laura

It took a while for the weather to break so that the grounds could hold their headstones. It was pretty surreal visiting my best friend and her brother at the cemetery. Now that their headstones were in place, this was my first time visiting their graves. I was still extremely fragile and sentimental. This wasn't supposed to be the end of their story. But *Anthony and Lea* were together again at last. And I knew that I did the right thing by having them buried next to each other.

I took their losses hard, I don't think that I've ever cried so much in my life but that's all that I'd been doing for the past five months since they've been gone. My tears were painting history on my cheeks every time I cried.

I placed a single rose in front of both of their headstones and squat down taking in a healthy breath of fresh air. I took off my black glasses and closed my eyes as a cool breeze grazed over my face. The breeze made my tears feel cold as they slowly melted down my cheeks. I had so much that I wanted to say to both Anthony and Lea. I had all of this money that Anthony had left me with, yet the hole in my spirit was unrepairable. Money could never heal the pain I was feeling. I think I'd lost all control of my inner peace. I haven't been able to eat or return to work because the grief was too unbearable.

I inhaled. "Where do I start?" I sniffed. I sat my bottom down in front of both headstones. It was time that I got some of this hurt off my chest. I turned towards Lea's headstone first.

"Hey sis. Damn, I miss you so much girl! So much has been going on, I swear, this still doesn't even seem real. It's like the world is moving but I'm standing still. I just can't wrap my mind around the fact that my best friend is really gone. I love you so much Lea and if you were still here, I would've been right by your side still getting on your nerves trying to force you to take your medication." I chuckled. Then I got serious again when I thought about lil' Anthony.

"Oh, I got great news that you'd actually be surprised about if you were still here. Apparently your mom made a promise Anthony that if anything had ever happened to you that she would take care of lil' Anthony. Well, she has fulfilled her promise. She's going through all the proper steps to get full custody of lil' Ant. He's been staying with her since you've been gone. They live in a big mansion out in New Hampshire and I talk to him every night to tell him I love him. I told him that you are in heaven and that you will always be with him everywhere he goes." I cried. I had to pull a piece of tissue out of my purse before I continued. "And although your mom and her husband has their own money, I gave them a substantial amount of money to contribute to lil' Ant's medication and college fund. As long as I'm breathing, I will always make sure that he knows who his mom was and how much you loved him. And I know it probably sounds strange, but the way that I see your mom loving on him, is probably the way she wishes she loved on both you and Anthony."

I inhaled and faced Anthony's gray, glossy headstone. Just thinking about how much he helped to change my life and shape my future had me immediately bursting out in tears. My words were stuck in my throat and I had to calm myself down. Anthony had so much promise, so much to offer to the world, but I understood that GOD wanted him more.

"Well Anthony, I guess I can finally reveal the crush that I've always had on you." I giggled and wiped my right tear with the back of my hand. "But on a serious note, I've always admired everything about you. I've never met anyone with a heart like yours. You stayed the same from when we were younger, till the day you left. I will never forget you Anthony, *ever*! I'm using the money you left me with to open up that car dealership that you talked about. I'm signing the lease for the location on Monday and business will be fully operating as soon as next month. I plan to donate the first four month's profit to a fund I created in your name to help inner city youth learn about opening businesses and managing their credit at an early age so that they won't try to make quick money on the streets. I'm just trying to make you proud and do what's in my heart with what you left me."

I paused before revealing the news that I heard about the cowards who set him up. "The court case is over. The judge threw the book at Ms. Antonia. Her ass will never see the light of day. Turns out, she had a vendetta against you the day Nicky took her own life. She was always plotting on a scheme to get back at you. And when she found out you were in prison with her nephews, Lim and Rico, she started writing you to keep you close so that her plan would come together. I heard that after you got out of prison and she got to know you when you lived with her, she changed her mind and called it off. But it was too late, Lim and Rico were already in too deep. Turns out, the rumors about her were true, that bitch was evil foreal! And apparently she had a reputation of being quick tempered and violent. Her scheme to use her nephews to do her dirty work, fucked all of their lives up because the judge gave Lim and Rico life in prison as well. And get this, they are both locked up in the same facility as J-Boy and Terror."

I stood up and dusted off the back of my summer dress to finish speaking to Anthony.

"I visited J-Boy and Terror just recently and I told them that I will always hold them down while they were in there, just like you would have done. They were grateful and they miss you like crazy too. They really took losing you hard Anthony, especially J-Boy. I could see revenge burning all in his eyes when he told me that Lim and Rico were housed in the same unit as he and Terror."

I placed my glasses back on my face and blew both Anthony and Lea a kiss. Before I could walk away, I almost forgot to deliver J-Boy's message.

"Oh, yeah, J-Boy wanted me to tell you that he was about to *'Put A Woke To Sleep'* just like he promised you he would. Whatever that's supposed to mean.

*****

Chapter 21

J-Boy

Location: Shirley Maximum Prison- Shirley, Massachusetts

I didn't give one fuck if a motherfucker in prison saw me shed tears. Anthony was my brother even before I knew that he was my blood brother. Hearing the news about him being murdered while I was in prison, hurt more than anything I've ever felt. That was my motherfuckin' nigga and I stood ten toes down with him. Riding for him went without saying. I told him not to trust them bitch ass nigga's Lim and Rico but my nigga had the kind of heart that he wished other niggas had. But a lot of these cowards out here ain't built like that.

I planned to show my nigga Ant, exactly what kind of heart I had. Lim and Rico were gonna' feel me! Every time I saw them niggas outside at rec, the fear in their eyes only fueled me to want to get at them sooner. The only reason that I hadn't already handled them was because Terror kept trying to talk me out of it. That shit shocked the fuck out of me. Terror was Ant's right hand man and we always did shit as a unit, but this nigga been spitting that '*he's changing*' shit, ever since Ant's been gone.

Today was the day that I was going to get Terror's mind right once and for all. I was leaning against the iron gate out at rec and he was standing beside me. We were in full view of Lim and Rico. I hated them niggas so bad, it was hard for me to even look in their direction. They were on the basketball court shooting hoops by themselves because nobody fucked with them because of what they did to Ant. I'm really surprised that they weren't in protective custody but I think their pride was holding them back from requesting it. They didn't want to look like punks. But I was glad they didn't, it only gave me free access to get at them. Most of the niggas in prison that knew Ant, knew that I planned to handle Lim and Rico and that's why they haven't been touched yet.

"A'ight so here's the plan. I got two blades from that old head last night. The one that told us that he knew Ant's pops. He gave me one for me and one for you. I didn't even have to pay him because nigga's want this shit done as bad as I do. So tonight, me and you are going to wait until Lim is inside of Rico's cell so that they are alone together. I'm gonna' have niggas looking out for the guards while we go in there. We are going to handle that shit and rock out of there. Simple as that. So what you gonna' do Terror, you riding for Ant or what?"

Terror shook his head. "Man, the old me would've handled them cowards the day they stepped foot in here. But Ant wouldn't have wanted that shit. We already let him down by landing ourselves in this bitch in the first place. Now you wanna' do some dumb shit to add to our sentences? Come on J, be smart, nigga. If anything, let these niggas in here that already got life sentences handle them. Think logically my nigga, it's time for you to change your shit up too."

"Oh so you think you Ant now? Trying to think logically and shit. Ant is dead man, and them niggas are the ones who killed him! If you let that shit ride, you just as guilty as them niggas are. I'm sick of you talking about this changing shit. You riding or what?" I jumped in Terror's face. We were now eye to eye.

"Nah'. Ant was my nigga, but this isn't the way he would have wanted us to ride for him."

I pushed Terror to the gate and it caught his fall. "Fuck you then nigga! You a straight BITCH for not riding for Ant!"

Terror didn't even hit me back, he lifted himself off the gate and he put his hands up. "Well then I'll be a bitch then J, but I'm not doing no stupid shit. And you better not either, we got too much to look forward to."

I took one last look into my nigga Terror's eyes and said, "FUCK YOU!" I turned my back against him and walked away.

"Don't do it J, Ant wouldn't have wanted that shit." He hollered out behind me. I waved him off and I continued to walk away. I spent the rest of the time at rec marinating on what I was going to do when we got back inside.

BEEP! BEEP! BEEEEEP!!!!

The alarm sounded off, alerting us that it was time to line up for roll call. We formed a line and the guards did their head count and escorted us back inside. When I got back to my cell, I laid on my bunk thinking. I was so angry at Terror for not wanting to rip the skin off of Lim and Rico with me. Them niggas didn't deserve to see another day. I thought about Terror's words and he reminded me of Anthony, trying to think logically and go another route. But it was too late for that. I wasn't in my right state of mind to be thinking rational. These niggas killed my brother and so I made up my mind that I was going to kill them.

Later that night, I stepped out of my cell and hit the common area. There was a bunch of niggas watching the Celtics game on the big TV, Lim was one of them. Rico had just left to go inside his cell when I was walking up. I saw the back of his head when he entered it. I stood in the cut waiting for Lim to get up to go follow behind him. It was a routine that they had been doing every night. Especially since they didn't have anyone else to talk to besides each other.

Finally Lim stood up and started walking in the direction of Rico's cell. I quickly sped to my room to get my blade and returned to the common area. I saw the old head who gave me the blade. I shot him a look to see if the coast was clear. He tilted his head up to give me the go-ahead and I immediately headed that way. I didn't see anything else but red as I marched towards Rico's cell. Vengeance was flowing through my veins and revenge was firing through my eyes. Both of them had to go!

When I got to the cell, Lim's back was facing me and Rico was sitting on the bed. They were talking and having a good ole' conversation. I couldn't wait to cut their conversation short. I pulled the blade out of the band of my pants and called Lim's name.

"Yo' Lim." He turned around and I immediately stuck him in the stomach as hard as I could. I forced the man-made blade so far into his stomach, with any more force, it would've came out through his back.

"What the fuck!" Rico shouted with his eyes full of fear. When Lim collapsed to the floor, I quickly jumped on Rico, pinned him to his bed and stuck him in his stomach over and over again. I gutted that coward like a pig. "This is for Ant nigga! You killed my fuckin' brother, you coward ass, bitch made nigga! Rest in PISS!" I spit in his face as his body laid lifeless.

I stood up and scoped out all of the blood on the bed, on their bodies, on the floor and all over me. I did it, and this shit was real. They took my nigga Ant for granted and they deserved what they had coming. Ant thought these niggas were so woke and so real and they ended up switching up on him and being the opps the whole time. Well I promised my nigga that I would lay a **WOKE NIGGA TO SLEEP** for him, and I fulfilled that. The monster in me had came out and presented itself with a vengeance and I couldn't even recognize myself. Once I walked out of Rico's cell and saw my nigga Terror, reality finally sank in. I saw him survey all the blood on my shirt and then he looked at the blade that I still had in my right hand and he nodded slowly. His eyes were full of disappointment and although revenge felt good, I knew that I had let both him and Anthony down.

"GET DOWN, DOWN ON YOUR KNEES!!!" The correctional officers rushed over and bombarded me to the ground. I still didn't take my eyes off of J-Boy while they were rushing me. The look on his face was as if he wanted to help me but he knew that there was nothing he could do about it. He probably felt like he was losing another brother. The officers cuffed me and took the blade out of my hand. When they lifted me up, I shouted out to Terror. "I'm sorry dog, I should've listened. I love you. Make Ant proud."

Terror shook his head and beat his heart with his fist. "You my brother. We crew for life." He said. It seemed like he was trying to fight back tears. It was over for me and he knew it.

Reflecting on how shit just went down, things didn't' go as planned. I was supposed to stick them niggas, make it back into my cell to change clothes, and pretend to be clueless. But that didn't happen. I didn't know where the correctional officers came out the cut from but I was prepared to accept my fate.

The officers fucked me up real bad before they put me in the hole. They slammed the door shut and was yelling all types of profanity before they locked me in. I sat inside on the floor. It was lonely, dark, dirty and cold. I was in so much pain but my heart was especially heavy. I shed hard tears and I said a prayer because I knew it was a done deal for me. There was no way that I'd ever see the light of day. I crawled up on the top bunk and used the shadow from the small rectangular window as a light to see the wall. I tapped the blood that was dripping on my face from the swollen black eye that the guards had just given me and I used it to write on the dingy white paint.

I wrote: *Ant, Leon, Terror and J-Boy... The Crew for life. I love you mom, I'm sorry*.

With tears in my eyes, I slid off my extra-large pants and tied one of the pant legs around my neck in a solid knot. I reached up to tie the other leg on the broken light fixture on the ceiling. I couldn't blame anybody else, I did this to myself and I didn't know how much I was going to regret it until now.

"GOD please forgive me." I said, and I jumped.

Chapter 22

Terror

My night was fucked up! I told J-Boy to chill but for him, revenge was the only option. That's usually how we handled things coming up so I understood his position. We always looked out for each other. But as grown men, we had to be more strategic with our decisions. When I saw him walking out of Rico's cell covered in blood, I knew that he executed his plan. But he wasn't thinking logically. The old head that he thought had his back, didn't even have niggas watching out to see if the guards were anywhere around, shit was done sloppy. I tossed and turned all night trying to stop blaming myself for what J-Boy did to Lim and Rico. But I also knew that I could've talked to J-Boy till I was blue in the face, there was no changing his mind. I had seven years left for my parole hearing and J-Boy had less than that, now, his future was bleak.

The next day, I adjusted my mindset to be ready to be locked down. When there were fights, stabbings or contraband found in any of the units, they'd lock down the facility and only let us out for two hours a day. Both Lim and Rico were dead so the unit would be locked down until further notice. All that lock down did was give niggas more time to think and more time to live inside of our heads, which isn't always a good thing. It made some niggas go crazy.

"SHAKE DOOOOWN!" The guards yelled out as they clicked the cells open and tore through our belongings like rats in a dumpster. Since J-Boy was found with a blade, the correctional officers had to make sure that there weren't any more blades or weapons in the entire unit.

I leaned against the wall outside of my cell as they searched through my belongings and destroyed most of my shit. This chubby light skinned officer that no one liked stood by the door overseeing them. He kept peeking over at me and then looking back into the room.

"What? You ain't gonna' find nothing in there. I don't know why you keep staring at me like that." I told him. I wasn't in the mood for the shenanigans.

He smirked. "Your friend is dead, he hung himself last night." He revealed nonchalantly.

"What, what are you talking about? Who?" I asked.

"Jamille Harold aka J-Boy, he's dead." Upon his last words, the rest of the officers exited my cell after not finding anything. The chubby officer walked off with them to search another cell and didn't offer any other information. That motherfucker didn't even offer his condolences! He didn't give a single fuck! He just told me that my motherfuckin' nigga was dead with no sympathy in his eyes or in his tone.

"Yo' Terror, I just heard what he said, I'm sorry to hear that dog." My cellmate said re-entering the cell with me.

"I appreciate that dog. But I just wanna' be left alone right now man."

"I respect that." He said, fixing the covers back on his mattress that was ripped off by the guards. I didn't give a fuck what was on my bed. I hopped up on my bunk and laid down on the bare, dirty mattress, turned toward the wall and shed tears for my nigga.

The next two weeks were the longest two weeks of my life. Imagine being locked in a room for twenty-two hours a day after finding out that one of your best friends just hung himself? We just recently lost Ant, this loss was just adding to the torture. I was mentally and emotionally fucked up. As much as I tried, it was too hard to declutter my mind.

First Leon, then Ant and now J-Boy, I was really the last man standing and I was left suffering.

Brothers often fought, argued and had disagreements, but at the end of the day, the love remained and that's what we shared. A bond that I'd never forget and will always remember. However, this empty space in my heart that my friends left me with, would never be filled. These losses left me grief stricken and paralyzed with depression. I missed my niggas, every, single, day.

Finally lock down was over and prison resumed back to its normal state.

"Tyrone Harris?" An older black correctional officer with a head full of gray hair stood by the door of my cell and looked at me. I sat up in my bunk.

"I'm Tyrone Harris, what's up?" I asked him.

He nodded. "I'm sorry about what happened to your friend." He said.

"Man, you don't give a fuck." I waved him off.

He scratched his beard and then folded his arms. "I'm not your enemy young brother, I was just offering my condolences; it's up to you to accept it. I know that you're going through a lot dealing with the loss of your friend but he made his own decision. I'm sure he wanted to get revenge because of what happened to your friend Anthony, I read about the story on the news. But you young brothers need to understand that the best revenge is success and love. Y'all young niggas always risking your freedom for all the wrong things."

"Yeah, whatever." I dismissed him.

"See what I'm saying, y'all don't listen. But anyway, you have a visitor."

"A visitor?" I quizzed.

"Yes, come on!" He demanded.

217

I followed behind the guard and was led to the visitor line. The correctional officers called out a few more names before leading us to the visiting room.

Standing at the table to greet me in a green summer dress with her hair pulled back in a neat ponytail was Laura. She looked like and angel standing there resembling the singer Keri Hilson. It was a breath of fresh air to see someone from the outside. She had visited me and J-Boy right after Ant died, but this time, her timing couldn't have been more perfect. She hugged me and the strawberry scent that she wore was welcoming.

She sat in her seat and her personality shined through her classy energy. "Hey Terror, I'm just coming up here to check up on you. I plan to come back and visit J-Boy next week to do the same. I've been making sure that I keep plenty of money on both of your books and I just wanted to make sure you guys didn't need anything." She smiled.

I couldn't speak, I was paralyzed in my seat and a tear fought its way out my left eye.

"Terror what's wrong?" Laura asked, bending her manicured eyebrows in concern.

"He's gone. J-Boy killed Lim and Rico and then hung himself."

"He did what?" She covered her mouth with both of her hands. Tears wasted no time falling from her eyes. "I'm so sorry." She cried.

"Everybody's gone Laura, my brothers are all dead. I don't have any family, no friends, I don't have no one! A nigga is *all* alone. It seems like right when a nigga wants to change his life, everything turns to shit. I don't have shit to live for anymore."

"Don't you dare say that! You have *everything* to live for. You mentioned change, and change starts with your mindset." She said as she pointed her pink fingertip to her temple. "Remember when we were all coming up, you, Ant and the crew were hanging tough and I was rolling with Lea and our little crew? We wanted to be like y'all so bad. We were

218

getting into fights and doing dumb shit because we didn't know any better. Well when I went to nursing school, I had to separate myself from a lot of the girls in order to get my mind right and head down a different path. I changed my mindset and I stayed focused and I lost a lot of friends in the process. What I'm trying to say is, sometimes you have to focus on yourself and you can't EVER give up."

"Man you sound like Ant."

Laura chuckled. "I guess he rubbed off on all of us. In a positive way." She reached over and grabbed my hand and stared me in the eyes. "Don't give up okay, I'm here for you."

"Thank you." I told her.

-7 years later

Terror

Location: Cedar Grove Cemetery, Boston Massachusetts

"My nigga, my nigga. Your right hand man is back out here!" I said standing in front of Anthony's grave. I nodded. "Dog, I miss you so fuckin' much." I smiled, reminiscing on old times. Although much time has passed by, it still feels like yesterday that the crew was all together, smiling, laughing and talking shit to each other.

I took in a deep breath, I had only been out on parole for six months and I was still adjusting to the outside world. Visiting Ant's grave was something I wanted to do sooner but my parole terms didn't allow it. I was instructed to go to work and spend the rest of the time on house arrest for six months. Now that it's over, coming to see my nigga was the first thing I did.

I looked down at his gray, glossy headstone. Reading his name etched on the stone was making a nigga feel sentimental. Getting out of prison and connecting with Ant and J-Boy as a family was supposed to be the move. Here I was, standing at the cemetery to visit my nigga. Shit wasn't right.

"I got some updates for you dog. I took your advice and gave up the street life. No more guns, no more hustling. I gave all that shit up! A nigga is a working man now. I got on my suit and shit looking smooth." I joked, fixing my gray tie and smoothing the pants on my black suit. "But on some real shit, smartest thing you could've ever done was leave Laura with that money. By the time I got out, she had opened five different dealerships in five different cities. All types of celebrities from rappers, actors and ball players order custom exotic cars from the dealerships. My parole officer had signed off for me to work at the Boston location and now that I'm off parole, I'm helping Laura run all of the locations remotely and sometimes on site. Which is why a nigga got this clean suit on." I laughed, wishing my nigga was around to witness how much I've change.

"Laura picks up your nephew every other weekend and brings him to the dealership so we can teach him the ropes early. Keep it in the family, that's what you always wanted right, my nigga?" I smiled. "He is healthy and happy. And you should see his eyes light up when I tell him stories about you. He's a teenager now and that little nigga looks just like you and he acts like you too with that big ass heart he has. I must say, your mom is doing a really good job taking care of him, I'm sure you'd be pleased. Oh and speaking of moms, I haven't seen you and J-Boy's mom since I been out. She won't even tell me where J-Boy is buried and that shit hurts." Tears bridged my eyes and I sniffed and looked away.

"I know that you, J-Boy and Leon are looking down and watching over me. Tell my niggas that we still Gang! Gang! Gang! And I love them!!" I chuckled. "I miss old times with the crew man, we had so much fun. And I really miss you. You were like a father figure to all of us since we didn't have one. And on dogs, it seems like messages be coming from you in the form of others. I remember a guard in prison said to me, *'the best revenge is through success and love'* and those words stuck with me because it was some shit that you would say. That shit was some of the truest shit ever spoken."

I smiled and looked up. "Come here baby." I said.

Laura placed a rose in front of Lea's headstone and came to stand beside me. I gripped her waist and pulled her towards me. "Ant, I want to say thank you for bringing Laura back into my life. She held a nigga down for seven years and we just got married." Laura smiled and held up her left hand toward the headstone. "Yes your boy is married, can you believe that shit Ant?" Laura and I shared a laugh and then we smiled toward the headstone. "This woman is amazing. She put 400 high school graduates through College using one of the foundations she created in your name and she makes it her duty to keep the money circulating in the community. So you didn't die in vain bro. None of this would've been possible without you."

Laura interrupted. "I also want to say thank you as well Ant. I have a great man, a secure future, I'm giving back and I couldn't be happier. So again, from the bottom of my heart, thank you Anthony." She stood to her tippy-toes and pecked me on the lips. "Oh and I made him retire the name Terror, his name is Tyrone, I call him by his real name because he's a professional now."

"Yea, yeah, yeah." I said smiling as I looked at my beautiful wife. Shorty was my Beyonce and I appreciated her so much. She had such a profound outlook on life and she helped me discover my purpose. I was now making it my duty to speak at prisons to talk to young men to keep them on the right path. I never thought in a million years that I would do some shit like this, but Laura made me feel good about giving back.

"*Success and love is the best revenge* and I have both now. Success *and* Love." I said to Ant. I took my hand and placed it on Laura's protruding belly. "You have a new niece on the way. I'm going to be a father dog. Isn't that shit wild? I'm finally going to have my own family." I smiled and then it disappeared as I put my head down. It hurt that my nigga wasn't around to share these moments with me. Laura wiped my tears with her bare hands and kissed me again.

"I'll let you finish talking to him babe, I'll go wait for you in the car. I love you." She embraced me and headed to sit inside our black Maybach.

I stared in her direction as she walked away. Something about her carrying my child made me love her that much more. "Dog, I hate to sound gay and shit, but I finally get to experience the kind of love that you used to talk about having with Nicky. You know my family situation has always been fucked up, but my wife makes up for all of that. She got that authentic love for a nigga and it feels good." I smiled thinking about how blessed I was. Things were finally starting to look up for me.

"Well my nigga, I don't want to talk your head off. I just wanted to mainly come here to say thank you for everything. For your guidance, your friendship and your brotherhood. I will never forget you. My right hand man Ant, you're a motherfuckin' legend!"

Suddenly a car rolled up and I turned to see who was inside the dark gray Chevy. A light skinned Fat Joe looking nigga that looked like he was walking with a cane; limped my way.

"What up Terror, this is for my family, The White Brothers. DIE SLOW NIGGA!"

POP! POP! POP! POP!

Fast shots darted into my stomach and chest and I collapsed to the ground instantly. I think I was more in shock than anything.

SKURRRTTT! The coward ass nigga limped back to his car and sped away fast.

I rubbed my chest and looked in the palm of my hand and it was covered in blood. I heard Laura crying and running towards me. She was screaming and telling me to stay awake.

She lifted me in her lap and tried to apply pressure to my wounds. "Somebody help me please!!! HELLLLP ME PLEAAAASE!!!" She cried louder.

She smacked me on the cheek to try to keep me awake. "Don't leave me baby, stay with me, stay with me Tyrone baby. It's going to be okay! You gotta' hold on, fight baby, fight through this!"

I was breathing heavily. The euphoria of being shot had me panicking because I had no control over my body. I fought to hold onto all of the small breaths I was able to take but I began choking on my blood. "HELPPPP MEEEEE! Somebody please, help me! My husband's been shot!" My wife shouted. She rocked me in her lap and her tears were landing on my face. "Stay with me baby, I can't lose you! Don't leave me out here alone! Me, my son and the baby can't lose you

Tyrone. I love you so much!" Laura screamed out at the top of her lungs. Her beautiful face was fading in and out of my vision. I felt myself rapidly deteriorating.

Nestled in the arms of the woman that I love, I reflected on my life. After all of the hard losses that I've taken, I finally got to experience love and it's beautiful emotion. Nothing in life felt better than having the love of a real woman and I knew that now. And although success and love was the best revenge, I guess that didn't matter when you still had smoke with cowards on the streets. After all these years, that nigga still couldn't let go of that beef that he had with Anthony because of what his pops did to the White Brothers. Anthony was already gone, but I guess it made this coward ass nigga feel better if the whole crew was wiped out, especially since Ant shot him up. Walking with that cane will be a constant reminder of that. But I guess I should've seen this coming. Beef in the hood didn't just disappear, no matter how much I wanted to change my life. It was always something, and you never knew which direction it was coming from. Damn!

I rolled my head towards Anthony's headstone and I whispered, "See you soon my nigga."

Suddenly, all of my breath left my body. Laura's cries faded out and the pain escaped me. I saw a bright white light flash before me and the crew were all on the other side of the light smiling largely and welcoming me. The light was so calming, and so serene. I felt a comfortable smile form on my face as I walked their way. Once I got to the end of the light, I felt free and all of my worries disappeared. The crew was back together at last.... *I'm sorry Laura, and thank for loving a nigga like me. Tyrone AKA Terror....*

RIP – The Bean Town CREW... Anthony, Leon, J-Boy & Terror...

BE SURE TO PICK UP THESE HOT RELEASES BY "THE QUEEN PENS"!!!

CPSIA information can be obtained
at www.ICGtesting.com
Printed in the USA
LVHW05s2017170518
577556LV00011B/637/P

9 781717 162632